Donald MacKenzie and The Murder Room

>>> This title is part of The Murder Room, our series dedicated to making available out-of-print or hard-to-find titles by classic crime writers.

Crime fiction has always held up a mirror to society. The Victorians were fascinated by sensational murder and the emerging science of detection; now we are obsessed with the forensic detail of violent death. And no other genre has so captivated and enthralled readers.

Vast troves of classic crime writing have for a long time been unavailable to all but the most dedicated frequenters of second-hand bookshops. The advent of digital publishing means that we are now able to bring you the backlists of a huge range of titles by classic and contemporary crime writers, some of which have been out of print for decades.

From the genteel amateur private eyes of the Golden Age and the femmes fatales of pulp fiction, to the morally ambiguous hard-boiled detectives of mid twentieth-century America and their descendants who walk our twenty-first century streets, The Murder Room has it all. >>>

The Murder Room
Where Criminal Minds Meet

themurderroom.com

Donald MacKenzie 1908–1994

Donald MacKenzie was born in Ontario, Canada, and educated in England, Canada and Switzerland. For twenty-five years MacKenzie lived by crime in many countries. 'I went to jail,' he wrote, 'if not with depressing regularity, too often for my liking.' His last sentences were five years in the United States and three years in England, running consecutively. He began writing and selling stories when in American jail. 'I try to do exactly as I like as often as possible and I don't think I'm either psychopathic, a wayward boy, a problem of our time, a charming rogue. Or ever was.'

He had a wife, Estrela, and a daughter, and they divided their time between England, Portugal, Spain and Austria.

By Donald MacKenzie

Henry Chalice
Salute from a Dead Man (1966)
Death is a Friend (1967)
Sleep is for the Rich (1971)

John Raven
Zaleski's Percentage (1974)
Raven in Flight (1976)
Raven and the Ratcatcher
  (1976)
Raven and the Kamikaze (1977)
Raven After Dark (1979)
Raven Settles a Score (1979)
Raven and the Paperhangers
  (1980)
Raven's Revenge (1982)
Raven's Longest Night (1983)
Raven's Shadow (1984)
Nobody Here By That Name
  (1986)
A Savage State of Grace (1988)
By Any Illegal Means (1989)
Loose Cannon (1994)
The Eyes of the Goat (1992)
The Sixth Deadly Sin (1993)

Standalone novels
Nowhere to Go (1956)
The Juryman (1957)
The Scent of Danger (1958)
Dangerous Silence (1960)
Knife Edge (1961)
The Genial Stranger (1962)
Double Exposure (1963)
The Lonely Side of the River
  (1964)
Cool Sleeps Balaban (1964)
Dead Straight (1968)
Three Minus Two (1968)
Night Boat from Puerto
  Vedra (1970)
The Kyle Contract (1971)
Postscript to a Dead Letter
  (1973)
The Spreewald Collection
  (1975)
Deep, Dark and Dead (1978)
The Last of the Boatriders
  (1981)

The Last of the Boatriders

Donald MacKenzie

An Orion book

Copyright © The Estate of Donald MacKenzie 1981

The right of Donald MacKenzie to be identified as the author of this work has been asserted in accordance with the Copyright, Designs and Patents Act 1988.

This edition published by
The Orion Publishing Group Ltd
Orion House
5 Upper St Martin's Lane
London WC2H 9EA

An Hachette UK company
A CIP catalogue record for this book is available from the British Library

ISBN 978 1 4719 0591 9

www.orionbooks.co.uk

For Edwina Mary Wood

Boatrider

In the days of the river boat gamblers, the professionals were known as boatriders. The meaning of the term changed over the years until in the 1930s it had become the generic term for travelling thieves who patronized ocean-going liners. The following twenty years saw yet another modification until today the term boatrider means no more or less than a con man afloat.

ONE

The slow-moving river was just visible from the study windows. Beyond the fringing osiers the sloping ground rose towards oak and chestnut trees. Straw littered the flower-beds in front of the windows, protecting the tulips and daffodils from ground frost. A straight half-mile of poplars made an avenue that ran to a gated bridge. White painted post-and-rail left and right of the driveway enclosed empty paddocks.

Philip Drury moved uncomfortably. White-haired and erect, he had lost no more than an inch in height in his adult years, and a generation spent in the saddle had kept his muscles reasonably hard. He wore grey tweeds with easy grace. His vowel sounds were Virginian.

'Come on, now, honey. It isn't the end of the world!'

'It's the end of *your* world,' said his daughter, staring at him from dark blue eyes. She had a small provocative face with ear-length honey coloured hair and a tilted nose. Her colouring and features were those of her dead mother, her attitudes Drury's.

He followed her look to the silver frames on the mantel. The thoroughbred horses in the photographs had represented the Haras Orbec in sales rings from Keenesland to Newmarket. Many of them had been painted by Skeaping and the faded patches on the walls showed where the frames had hung.

The auction that had been held the previous week followed the forced sale of the mares, foals and yearlings. Everything that Drury had worked for over the past twenty-five years now belonged to the Banque Ottomane.

Everything. The timbered manor house and barns, thirty loose-boxes and one hundred and fifty hectares of lime-nourished grassland.

Judy Ashe dragged her eyes from the blank screens of the closed-circuit television system. Cameras had once controlled the foaling boxes night and day, scanning the newly born animals as they sprawled under the heat-lamps. It had been enough then to say the name of the Orbec Stud to see respect dawn on people's faces. She shook her head and pitched her cigarette at the apple logs burning in the fireplace.

'I just don't understand it, Papa. How *could* things go so wrong, I mean so *completely* wrong?'

It was too late to tell the truth about so many things, especially to her. He moved into the explanation that practice had made almost perfect.

'It doesn't take that much understanding, Judy. Not if you think about greed. If your mother had been alive it would never have happened.'

Her face tightened. 'You're damn right! She wouldn't have *allowed* it to happen.'

The heat from the fire was burning the backs of his legs and he moved out of range.

'I should never have gone into real estate. I wonder I survived as long as I did in a world full of pimps and sharks.'

She moved, making a small sound of frustration. 'I can't tell you how much I hate it. All my life I've been admiring the things that you've done, the way you created this place from scratch. I've always been proud of what the Haras Orbec stood for and to see it all go ... '

'We'll come out of it,' he answered.

'But this was my *home*!' she burst out. 'We're sitting in an empty house, don't you realize that, Papa? There's nobody here, not a single soul but you and me. And you stand there looking as though nothing has happened!'

He half smiled. 'And how do you suggest that I should look?'

'Like a man who's just seen his life's work go, that's how!'

Her outburst came as no surprise. There too she was like her mother, ready to say whatever was on her mind.

'Ah well,' he said, 'it's a good job there's a daughter to come to the aid of her ageing father.'

'Ageing nothing,' she snapped. 'What I have to deal with is a sixty-five-year-old child and an obstinate one at that.'

She had arrived at Orbec the previous evening after numerous phone calls and a week of evasion on his part. With the exception of what had been left in two of the bedrooms and the study, all the furniture and carpets had been sold at auction along with the paintings and bronzes. The bank had given him a month to vacate the premises. A removal van would collect the last of his belongings which would go into storage. He checked his watch and emptied a jug of water on the fire. Acrid steam rose in the chimney.

'Right,' he said, looking around for the last time. 'We might as well make a move.'

He stowed his bags in the boot of Judy's red Honda. His heavy baggage stood in the hallway, ready to be collected with the rest of his possessions. He locked the solid, nail-studded entrance door behind them and put the key in an envelope together with five hundred francs, a farewell gesture to the lodge-keeper. The great barns were still piled high with straw and hay. Birds had nested in the loose-boxes and stray hens were scratching around in the dirt near the water troughs. The empty paddocks were silent in the pale sunshine and if you listened hard it was possible to hear the sound of the distant river.

An impatient bleep on the horn broke the spell. He climbed into the car beside his daughter, taking no notice of the *Please Fasten Your Seatbelt* sign attached to the dash.

'Stop at the lodge,' he said, showing her the envelope. 'I need to drop this off.'

3

The Honda moved down the driveway. A *Slow for Horses* sign stood in the grass by the side of the open gate. Drury slipped the envelope through the lodge letter-box and walked away quickly without looking back. They were fifteen kilometres along the road to Boulogne before Judy spoke again, her voice irritated.

'Aren't you going to speak to me or what?'

He allowed himself a sideways glance. 'What do you want to speak about, honey?'

Her mouth tightened with exasperation. 'My God, but you're infuriating at times! Twenty-five years have just gone down the drain and you're sitting there grinning away like some damn Buddha! Just how much money *is* there left?'

He picked his way round the question like a cat crossing a wet yard. 'Not too much, I'm afraid.'

She put her foot down hard on the accelerator, overtaking a lumbering truck. She drove as she did most other things, totally committed once her decision had been taken.

'I want to know how you intend to live,' she demanded.

He was staring out at the countryside he had learned to love. 'I've still got a few irons in the fire.'

She went after him like a mosquito. 'What about your friends, people like Tim Wayburn? God knows you helped him. There must be *someone* in the racing world who'd be darned glad to have you. You're a better judge of a horse than any of them.'

'I'd say I'm as good as most,' he said carelessly. He turned his head and smiled. 'All I'm short of is a couple of million bucks.'

It was the lunch-hour and traffic was light, she took her eyes off the road momentarily.

'You still haven't answered my question, Papa. I asked you how much money is left.'

The facts were depressingly familiar. There were twenty-eight thousand dollars in a Swiss account, money that the Banque Ottomane knew nothing about, and that was it. He told her as much.

'Of course the money from your mother's life insurance is still intact and gathering interest,' he lied.

She shook her head. 'We're talking about you not me. I have all the money I need.'

It was true. Divorce from Julian Ashe had left her with a house and a sizeable cash settlement. She'd studied at the Slade for two years and turned her loft into a studio. Her pictures of horses were just beginning to sell. The knowledge did nothing to ease his conscience. He laid his hand on her knee.

'Don't worry, honey, I'll bounce back. We're going to start all over, maybe not in France or England but somewhere.'

'*We're* going to start all over?'

It was wishful thinking on his part. 'I meant *I* am. All I need is the time to get things straight in my head. I need to get away for a while. I need a change of pace. A cruise, maybe.'

The tickets were already in one of his bags, bought in Paris and paid for under a *nom de plume*.

Judy's mood changed suddenly. She pursed her lips and blew him a kiss. It was three o'clock local time when they drove on to the hovercraft. An hour and a half later they were driving up the M20 towards London. Judy's two-storey house was five hundred yards from Wimbledon Common in a peaceful backwater where children could still play safely on long summer evenings.

Drury unfastened the gate and held it open as his daughter drove her car into the roomy garage. There was a nursery suite built above the garage for the child she had never had. The Queen Anne replica had been erected in an acre and a half of grass and beech trees. Drury had always loathed Julian Ashe, a stockbroker with a strange sadistic mind. Judy had broken all links with him after the divorce and the decision entailed dropping most of their mutual friends and acquaintances. People, Judy announced, would have to take her on her own terms or not at all. It left her with no real ties and she was given to quixotic departures, closing her house and heading for wherever fancy might take her. Drury's hopes and plans for her ran together. She was still young and attractive.

He carried his bags into a hallway hung with old hunting prints. They had been a wedding present from him along with the Herring that was upstairs. The sitting room was bright with old-fashioned chintz covers and curtains. A jar of freesias stood on the piano. A Portuguese woman kept the place spick and span. He took his bags up to the room that was always his. Aluminium steps on the landing gave access to Judy's studio. Skylights had been cut in the roof. He put his things away in the Victorian mahogany wardrobe. The windows looked out over new grass beginning to grow through the winter-brown lawn. The resident blackbird scuttled away as Drury watched. A current copy of the *Bloodstock Breeders' Review* had been placed on the bedside table with a box of crystallized ginger. She wasn't missing a trick.

He went down to the kitchen and found Judy just about to fix herself a drink. He took the bottle and glass and added ice and lemon to her Campari.

'I do believe that you're enjoying all this,' he challenged.

'If I am it'll soon wear off,' she said and leaned back against the box of herbs growing on the window-sill.

'Come on now,' he kidded. 'You know you like having someone to worry about.'

Her eyes were serious. 'You're sixty-three years of age and incapable of taking proper care of yourself. I worry about you but I certainly don't enjoy it.'

'I won't be in your hair for long, honey,' he said and poured himself a scotch and water. 'There are things to be taken care of.'

'So you said.' She opened the glass door to the garden and threw out some crumbs for the blackbird. She closed the door again. It was March and still chilly. 'There are no strings here, remember. You're your own boss entirely.'

'Can I entertain lady friends?' He kept his face straight.

She looked at him for a while and then shook her head. 'God help the woman who gets involved with you. You've been in love with a horse ever since I can remember.'

She put their empty glasses into the sink. 'I have to go up to the studio. We'll eat at eight, peppered steak with mushrooms.' She pulled a smock over her head. 'Will you be all right?'

He nodded abstractedly, looking out at the gathering shadows. His favourite scotch, peppered steak and the *Breeders' Review*. It looked as if she was buttering him up for a long stay. He went through to the sitting room and waited until he heard her climbing the steps to the studio. There were three telephones in the house. The one facing him had an extension to Judy's bedroom. The studio phone was on a separate line.

He closed the door, sat on the sofa and picked up the phone. The small Bechstein had been his wife's. Her portrait hung above the fireplace. Most of the other things in the room he had known all his life. The faded relics of Virginian gentility, an inkwell fashioned from the hoof of his grandfather's favourite hunter. In a strange way this house made him feel uncomfortable. There were too many souvenirs of the past.

He dialled and the number rang for some time without answering. The office must be closed. He dialled again, changing the code and number. This time the response was immediate. It was years since he had heard the voice but he recognized it straightaway.

'Phil Drury,' he said.

The seconds ticked away as though Drury's caller was trying to place the name. Then came the answer.

'Phil! This is a surprise!'

'Hi!' said Drury. 'I'd like to see you some time tomorrow if that's possible.'

A note of reticence crept into the other man's professional heartiness.

'Great, the thing is, Phil, I don't have my diary with me. Where are you speaking from?'

'I'm in London, Wimbledon. I won't waste much of your time.'

'It's not that, Phil. Look, can you give me a hint?'

'I'd rather not,' answered Drury.

'I haven't touched any criminal work in twenty years,' said Vogel.

It was probably true. Vogel had used his time cleverly, changing his image of a hotshot police court lawyer to a specialist in insurance.

'This is something personal,' said Drury.

Vogel's voice relaxed. 'How about a quarter past ten? I'm pretty sure that I've nothing until just before eleven.'

'That'll be fine,' said Drury. Vogel was making himself very clear. Not too long for old clients with personal problems. 'Are you still at the same address?'

'Still there,' Vogel said heartily. 'I'll look forward to seeing you, Phil.'

Drury put the phone down thoughtfully. It was ironic that Vogel should be so anxious to forget the past. He was Drury's only real link with it.

He lit a lamp and read until Judy came downstairs to prepare the supper.

He woke early, his ears straining for the sound of the stud-groom's Volkswagen. Michel always superintended the morning feeds. An electric milk-cart whined up the road, jerking Drury's mind into the present. It was still dark, almost seven o'clock by his watch. The house was completely quiet, Judy's door closed. He showered and dressed in the same grey tweeds. Once he had shaved, he unlocked the smallest of his suitcases. Inside was a blue and white Danish-Lloyd folder containing a voucher for two tickets on a spring cruise aboard the M.V. *Skagerrak*. The voucher was in the name of Pachabell Limited. The cost of the two tickets was four thousand eight hundred and ninety pounds. Attached to the folder was a typed itinerary.

CARIBBEAN SPRING CRUISE

March 5	Leave Heathrow for Miami (British Airways)
March 6	Miami, resting period.
March 7	Sail aboard M.V. *Skagerrak* from Dodge Island Terminal
March 8	At sea
March 9	At sea
March 10	Port-au-Prince, Haiti
March 11	San Juan, Puerto Rico
March 12	At sea
March 13	At sea
March 14	St John's, Antigua
March 15	At sea
March 16	Barbados
March 17	Trinidad
March 18	At sea
March 19	Caracas, Venezuela
March 20	At sea
March 21	Georgetown, Grand Cayman
March 22	Georgetown, Grand Cayman
March 23	At sea
March 24	Kingston, Jamaica
March 25	Paradise Island, Bahamas
March 26	Paradise Island, Bahamas
March 27	At sea
March 28	Miami, return to Heathrow, London (British Airways) for European-bound passengers

Danish-Lloyd's M.V. *Skagerrak* has a gross tonnage of 25,000. Length 645 ft, cruise capacity 630. All suites and staterooms are outside and equipped with private bath, air-conditioning, radio and telephone. There is a doctor and hospital on board. Payment for purchases made on the ship is by means of vouchers redeemed by the passenger at the close of the cruise. All major credit cards are accepted. Hastrupbank offers you all normal banking services between 9 a.m. and 12 noon and between 2 p.m. and 5 p.m.

Ship-to-shore telephone permits you to call anywhere in the world while in port or at sea. The radio room offers a twenty-four hour service for telephonic and cable communication. Incoming letters, packages and cables are delivered to your stateroom as soon as possible after reception on board.

He put the voucher in his pocket and went downstairs. There were some letters on the hallway floor and a copy of *The Times.* He boiled eggs, made toast and coffee and carried a tray upstairs. He opened Judy's room, put the tray down and let in daylight. She was still asleep with one arm thrown across her face. Her bedroom was oddly childish with its shelves of Dickens, Thackeray and Robert Louis Stevenson. There were pony club rosettes and old school photographs. A silver-backed hairbrush and a couple of scent bottles were her only concessions to maturity.

He fanned her face with the newspaper. 'Wake o beloved for the dawn is rising!'

She removed her arm from her face and opened one eye after another. 'God,' she said sleepily. 'I'd forgotten how repugnant you can be first thing in the morning.' She glanced at her meal then let it fall to the floor.

He sat on the end of the bed, balancing his plate on his knees. Genes and environment had produced strange similarities of behaviour in them. They both discouraged kissing on the mouth. Both walked furiously in times of emotional stress and, tritely enough, neither could eat the white of a boiled egg.

She sat up in the bed, showing shoulders that were still slightly suntanned.

'I have to be in the West End at ten-fifteen,' he said.

She nibbled a piece of toast. 'Take the car,' she said indifferently, 'I don't need it.'

He shook his head. 'Too many problems with parking. I have to see a lawyer on business.' He was building a springboard for future activities.

She made a face over her coffee cup. 'What happened to those fine old principles, "Never trust a lawyer or a Buick driver"?'

'I'll be back in time for supper,' he said.

'You're your own boss,' she said, putting her cup on the tray and stretching. 'Come and go as you please. There's plenty of food in the freezer. I'll be up in the studio all day, the light should be good.'

'I have to see this lawyer about the money from your mother's insurance.' He was on dangerous ground but he forced himself to cover it.

She cocked her head on one side. 'I thought the bank took care of all that.'

'They do,' he said. He could count on one hand the occasions when he had lied to her and despised himself for doing it but he had to buy time. 'There's this scheme I heard about. Stock options with a fantastic tax umbrella. The only thing is that it might mean tying up that part of your capital.'

She locked her arms behind her head, looking at him. 'How many times do I have to tell you that I don't give a damn what happens to that money. People gamble on somebody's death and call it life insurance. I hate the idea.'

He shrugged. 'I'm going to confirm that cruise booking while I'm out this morning. How do I get to the nearest bus stop?'

She swung her long legs out of the bed. They stood close together as she showed him the way. She was still at the window when he looked back from the road.

A groundsman was seeding the grass in the middle of Vincent Square. Very few of the surrounding houses were used as homes. Most of them were occupied by consulting engineers, lawyers and various esoteric organizations. Daffodils were growing in the window-boxes in front of number six. The name *Vogel, House and Merryweather Solicitors* appeared on a beautifully polished brass plate.

Drury climbed the thickly carpeted stairs without haste. Life had left him fitter than most men of his age but he still believed in conserving his energy. The room at the top of the stairs looked like a display stand at the Design Centre; flocked wallpaper, tubular steel furniture and glass tables littered with expensive magazines. A girl rose from behind her typewriter.

'Mr Drury? Will you come this way, Mr Vogel is expecting you.' She held the door open invitingly.

Vogel's room faced the playing fields. Beyond these rose the Byzantine mass of Westminster Cathedral. Vogel stood, swollen by the years of high living but retaining the colouring and bearing of his Hanoverian ancestors. He was fitted out in a conservatively cut suit of charcoal grey flannel and wore a clove carnation in his buttonhole.

Drury took the outstretched hand. Nothing had changed about the short firm grip, the level gaze that was designed to inspire confidence. And, of course, the obligatory hint of humour.

'Phil, you old rascal! Sit yourself down! God, but it's good to see you after all this time.'

There was no law library, no pink-tied briefs. In their place were *Dun and Bradstreet*, prestige publications from the world of high finance and insurance. An Augustus John painting hung over the Adam fireplace and the phones blinked instead of ringing.

Drury lowered himself into a chair, remembering another office and a younger Vogel, completely amoral and deadly with brain and tongue. Henry Vogel had promised himself that he would be the highest paid criminal lawyer in London before he was thirty-five. He had succeeded. It was a measure of his sense of survival that he had known when to change his ground.

Vogel pushed a cigar box in Drury's direction. 'Do you still use these things?'

'Not at this hour of the morning.'

Vogel's slate coloured eyes were innocent. 'Where are you based these days, still in Normandy?'

'No,' said Drury. 'I sold out a couple of months ago. I'm staying with my daughter.' Vogel would have known about the sale of the stud, but protocol required bad news to be ignored unless the subject was broached by the victim.

'So what can I do for you, Phil?' Vogel placed his fingertips together.

'I've been trying to locate Mark Russell. He seems to have gone up in smoke.'

The name brought a frown to the lawyer's florid face. 'I've been out of touch with the mob for years, Phil. The last time I heard of Russell was eighteen months ago. Somebody said that he was working as a hotel porter. To tell the truth, I never much liked him. I never knew a gambler you could trust.'

'He was his own worst enemy,' said Drury.

'A fool,' answered Vogel. 'I mean to get the money you two did with never a hand raised in anger. They just don't operate like that any more. There's no one around but a bunch of hoodlums.'

Drury's grin was non-committal. 'You wouldn't have an address for Mark?'

'An *address*?' The word sounded almost obscene the way the lawyer said it. 'Good God, no! I couldn't even guess where he is. What do you want him for in any case? I thought all that went out of the window twenty-five years ago.'

'I've owed him money too long,' said Drury. 'It sounds as though it's a good time to repay it.'

Vogel lifted his hands. 'I wish I could help, Phil. Why don't you try that friend of his, the Canadian woman. She'd know if anyone does.'

'A good idea, but I don't know where she lives either.'

'She'll be in the book,' Vogel said breezily. He looked at his watch and came to his feet. 'You'll have to excuse me, Phil. I've got someone coming in in a couple of minutes. Drop by whenever you're in town.' His door closed before Drury had reached the landing.

He checked the secretary's phone book but there was no listing for Emily-May Hurran. He had more luck at the public library in Buckingham Palace Road. A girl in the reference section lent him a current copy of *Who's Who in America*. An entry gave him the lead that he wanted.

HURRAN Emily-May, author. b. Aug. 11 1920 York Mills Ontario Canada. Educ. St. Joseph's Convent School, Riverdale, Ontario. University of Toronto and Heidelberg. M.A. D. Litt. Numerous publications in Canada, the United States and United Kingdom. Pubrs. Macmillan and Houghton Mifflin Company. Address 18 Carboy Street Battersea London S.W. U.K.

Drury returned the book and used the public telephone in the entrance, giving the operator the name and address. Her reply was uncompromising.

'I'm sorry, caller, the number is ex-directory.'

'You mean it's unlisted?'

'The number is ex-directory,' she repeated.

He put the phone down and walked out to the street. It was just after eleven o'clock. Much of the London he remembered had vanished. This new city had a vulgar vitality that was as much North American as European. A young policeman with a beard and a walkie-talkie set clipped to his belt told Drury how to get to Battersea. He took a bus to the south side of the park and walked west past the gloomy Victorian mansion blocks. The address he wanted was in a short street of Georgian artisans' dwellings. Soaring property values had transformed these into 'bijou residences' with brightly painted front doors. Stone animals were cemented to doorsteps. The back gardens were decorated with *trompe-l'œil* vistas and each house bore some form of burglar alarm. Emily-May had an elegant entry-phone at the side of her yellow door. Drury pressed the buzzer and bent down. A voice rattled in the speaker.

'Yes, who is it?'

'Phil Drury.'

There was a long pause then the voice replied. 'Go away, Phil Drury, you're dead.'

'Stop fooling around and open up, Emily-May,' he insisted.

Two locks and a length of chain were unfastened and the door was opened by a woman with tinted grey hair worn loose about her handsome face. She was wearing a lavender coloured dress and buckled shoes and her eyes were warm and lively. She pulled Drury into an embrace that smelled of Paco Rabanne and kicked the door shut. Then she pushed Drury at arms' length and held him there, clinging onto his hands.

'Let me take a good look at you, you horrible man! How long has it been, six – seven years and nary a damn letter?'

She hurried him through a doorway into a room lined on three sides with bookshelves. The windows looked onto the street. Sofa and armchairs were covered with Ontario patchwork and there was a set of birch-framed paintings of yachts out on Lake Huron. Magazines littered the floor where they had been dropped. It was a comfortable room, a room used and lived in. Only when they were sitting side by side on the sofa did she release his hand.

He placed it over his heart. 'I thought about you, Emily-May.'

She snorted. Her teeth were well cared for and her own. 'You can slice that as thin as you like and it's still boloney.'

'It's God's truth, Emily-May,' he affirmed. 'You know very well why I never got in touch.'

'Ah!' It was at once an expression of affection and irritation. 'You mean the little monster.'

'I mean the little monster,' he agreed. 'I just couldn't watch him pissing his life away, Emily-May. And it's typical of course that he should get the last laugh. I was wiped out myself three months ago. It wasn't Mark's sort of gambling but it was bad enough. I got involved in real estate. They finished me in less than a year.'

She laid a ringless hand across his mouth. 'Coffee,' she said. She was back with a tray and cups and a percolator that she plugged into a wall socket. 'Now you can tell me everything,' she said, settling down beside him again.

'Well,' he said. 'Helen died four years ago and I guess that sort of kicked out the jams. I wasn't thinking right.'

She lit an oval Balkan Sobranie. 'I don't know why I didn't snatch you myself.'

'I snore?'

She moved her head. 'No, I had to go for a black-hearted little fraud who thinks that he's a judge of horseflesh. God *damn* him, Phil!'

He grinned. She was feisty, loyal and highly intelligent in most areas. Her weakness had always been a romantic interest in rogues. She had met Mark Russell in a bar in Acapulco twenty-seven years before. Twelve hours later they were lovers. Emily-May was no reformer. She listened spellbound to Russell's accounts of high life on the seamy side, her eyes filled with vicarious excitement. Theirs was a relationship that had tottered down the years, each of them seemingly satisfied with the status quo.

'Mark's like me, old,' he said.

'Rubbish!' she barked. 'I wish to God that he was like you. You're a survivor.'

'Not any more,' he said. 'At least not by myself. I need Mark, Emily-May.'

She drew deep on her cigarette, her eyes fixed on Drury. 'Let me tell you a few things about Mark Russell. In the first place I haven't seen the little bum in four months. *You* know how I loved that man! *Still* love him. My mistake was to give him money, two thousand pounds to pay off his debts, he said. Straighten things out. He took the money and never forgave me for giving it to him. It went

16

the way that everything else has gone, up the ass of some racehorse. Do you know what he's doing now?'

'Vogel told me. Night porter in some hotel or other.' He put his coffee cup on a side table.

She frowned. 'Not quite, but then not much better. He's night receptionist at the Orbus Hotel, a Paddington fleabag patronized by low-class Arabs and the local hookers. He gets twenty-five pounds a week, kebab twice a day and a cot somewhere up in the rafters. Can you imagine it, Phil, I offered him his room back upstairs but he wanted to skewer me. He claimed that I was too demanding! Now what in hell would you need him for?'

He understood her frustration, oh but he understood! 'I need him for the same reason that he needs me, Emily-May. I want to get him on his feet again, working. We've got to make that one last score before we kick it.'

She reacted strangely, leaning forward with shining eyes. 'The last caper.'

'If you insist,' he said fondly. 'Though no one's used "caper" since the days of James Bond.'

She paid him no heed, embarked on a flood of imagination. 'The last of the boatriders! Marble-fleshed and stiff, maybe, but they still have it where it counts.'

'Good God!' he said, looking at her. 'I do believe that you're serious.'

'You're damn right I'm serious,' she answered.

'I've done two things in my life,' he said. 'One of them's gone. There *is* nothing else for me, Emily-May.'

She took the coffee set out to the kitchen. When she returned it was obvious that she had been thinking.

'Where's the front money coming from?'

A look of displeasure spread across his face. 'You're beginning to sound like some broad in a gangster movie. I've still got a few thousand bucks that my creditors don't know about. They're tucked away in a Swiss account.'

Her hand rested briefly on his. 'If you're ever really in need . . .'

He took his hand away. 'What's the matter, you want

to support the pair of us? No Emily-May, but thanks just the same.'

'What happened to that daughter of yours?' she demanded.

His face for once was unsmiling. 'She got married and divorced. I'm staying with her as a matter of fact.'

She wasn't about to let him off the hook so easily. 'How much does she know about your past?'

The thought depressed him profoundly. 'Not a damn thing. The worst is that I've used money that belongs to her, Helen's life insurance policy. That's why this thing *has* to work, Emily-May. I'm only going to get one bite at the apple.'

She nodded understanding. 'So what's your plan?'

For him, acceptance of the inevitable had come eleven weeks ago. He had thought of little else since.

'Currency controls have gone all over Europe. People can move their money around freely. The loot's there for the taking.'

'It's just as well that Mark never was seasick.' She ground out her cigarette.

'It could be his one big chance. Our *last* chance.'

She made a quick gesture towards him. 'For God's sake, I'm not trying to stop you! You could be saving my life!'

'You!' He laughed. 'Not on your tyntype. You've got the world in front of you.'

'Stuff and nonsense! I haven't written a word worth shit in two years. I sit here asking myself what in hell I'm doing here living like this and the answer is always the same. I'm cutting my own throat. The plain truth is that I need Mark and he needs me but the way things are at present neither is any good to the other.'

'It'll all change once he's got some money again,' he promised. 'Do you think you could stop him gambling?'

'He stopped that a year ago.' Her eyes grew wistful. 'You probably think of me as a stupid old broad. I am. I gave Mark money to pay his debts and he holds it against me. I ruined his life, he says. If it hadn't been for me he'd have been in the Hall of Fame and I'm not so damn sure that he doesn't believe it. I want him back, Phil. Shifty, lovable little creep that he is, I want him back. But with his self-respect restored. That's the difference, you never lost yours.'

He glanced away, embarrassed by the turn of the conversation. 'What sort of shape is he in physically?'

She moved her shoulders. 'OK. He's still overweight and he's getting hard of hearing, but he's OK.' She took a folder of colour photographs from a drawer and gave them to Drury. 'These were taken in Sicily two years ago, just before the Maestro decided that my presence was inimical to his well-being.'

Drury leafed through the pictures. Russell's hair had finally gone leaving no more than a ginger-white fringe. His small fat body was clad in a natty summer suit. Two-inch heels brought his head level with Emily-May's chin. Drury gave the folder back.

'OK, so he's not gambling. How about the drinking?'

Emily-May turned her mouth down. 'I wouldn't think so, not unless they're crazy enough to leave him with the keys to the bar. You wouldn't have liked what you saw these last few years, Phil. He's either pawned or sold everything he owned. There's a bag upstairs with those priest's clothes and that's literally all that's left here. He's a sad belligerent little man and he blames it all on me. Please let me come with you.'

He straightened his spine very carefully. 'To the hotel? No, Emily-May, you can't do that to him.'

'I'm talking about this cruise, not the hotel.' Suddenly it was a small girl speaking. 'You say this is your last chance. It could be mine as well. *Please* Phil.'

He needed old friends around him and knew that this was only a token objection.

'You don't know what you're saying.'

Her manner changed again as though she sensed victory. 'No more windy arguments. It's settled. I pay my own expenses and that's that. It might even add a note of respectability to the proceedings.'

He laughed in spite of himself. 'You're an impossible girl, Emily-May. Come on, I'll buy you lunch.'

They ate in a Thameside pub, sitting on a jetty twelve feet out above the water. He showed her the cruise brochure and told her what he had in mind. The debris of the crab she was eating piled up on her plate as she listened. She picked up the cruise itinerary and read it through.

'"Resting period" – in Miami? What *can* they mean?'

'I'm up on the Sun Deck. The Scottsville Express is two decks below.'

She wiped her mouth with her handkerchief. 'He won't like that one little bit. He still has a very well-developed sense of his own importance.'

He dropped a shred of crabmeat through the cracks in the planks. A fish swirled and the morsel vanished. Emily-May was scribbling on a pad she had produced from her bag.

'The *Skagerrak*. I'm going to call American Express the moment I get home.'

He looked at her, remembering so many good times. He felt a whole lot better having talked to her and was secretly glad that she was coming with them.

'You're quite sure that you want to go through with this?'

She put her head on one side like a bird that hears an unfamiliar sound.

'You've known me a long time, Phil Drury. I don't say yes and mean no. What's worrying me right now is whether I'll be able to get a cabin.'

'You should have no problem,' he assured her. 'They were complaining in Paris that they were underbooked.'

She shivered. It was too cold to be eating outside. Only one other couple had followed their example.

'I'll get the bill,' he said and caught the waiter's eye.

Emily-May used her lipstick and smiled. 'You still haven't worked it out, have you, Phil?'

'What am I supposed to work out?'

She put her lipstick away and her elbows on the table. 'I want Mark. I want him in the house where I can see him. I want to belong, Phil. Screw marriage, I'm a romantic.'

He walked her back as far as her door. She touched his cheek with her fingertips.

'You are one sweet man and I'm glad that we found you again. Call me just as soon as you've seen Mark. And bring him back, Phil, dead or alive.'

The address that she gave him was a square near Paddington Station. The area had the seediness that attaches to the neighbourhood surrounding a railway terminus in any large city. The hotel was approached by a street of curtained doorways that gave access to Adult Sex Shows and Take Your Own Photographs Nude Model Studios.

A strong odour of burned fat emanated from the fried fish and kebab parlours. Cider drinkers sprawled on the pavements. The Orbus Hotel had been converted from three Victorian mansions. The paint had flaked over the entrance and the steps were stocked with dirty milk bottles. A sign hanging crookedly inside the glass door read *Sorry no singles*.

The lobby was drab with dingy brown curtains and carpet and smelled of stale tobacco smoke. The girl at the reception desk had her back turned to the street as she sorted mail into slots. She turned, hearing Drury's voice, a dusty blonde with a German accent. A card on the counter confirmed her nationality. *Inge Hofmeister*.

'Good afternoon, sir, may I help you?'

'I'm looking for Mister Russell,' he said. His old friend had wandered afar. Years ago he wouldn't have set foot in a fleapit like this.

Miss Hofmeister's eyes were smudged with fatigue and she wore a light moustache of sweat. She glanced down at the register.

'Do you know which room he is in?'

'He's not a guest,' said Drury. 'My understanding is that he works here.'

Miss Hofmeister's interest waned visibly. 'I am sorry but I do not know where this gentleman is.'

'Well he lives here, doesn't he?' Drury asked. 'Which is his room?'

The German's girl's mouth was thin. 'You will find it at the top of the house, through the fire-doors, number three.'

Drury nodded his thanks. Russell had never been averse to a sly grope where feasible. This would explain his marked lack of popularity. The lift was marooned on an upper floor and Drury was obliged to walk up five storeys stacked with dirty bed-linen and sacks of garbage. The fire-doors opened onto an uncarpeted landing with curtainless windows. The so-called rooms were no more than cubicles with an iron mesh instead of a ceiling. Drury tapped on the door and turned the handle.

Russell lowered his newspaper very slowly. He was lying on a cot in his underwear with a half-empty bottle of Indian Pale Ale on the floor within reaching distance. There was just enough space for a flimsy wardrobe, a chair and the bed. A canvas bag lay beneath the unframed mirror.

'Well,' said Russell, half-rising and assuming a theatrical expression of surprise. 'If it isn't the Sage of Normandy!'

Drury took the one chair. 'Hi!' he said cheerfully and nodded at the mesh overhead. 'Are we allowed to talk or have you lost your privileges?'

'There's nobody here except me,' said Russell. 'How did you find this place?'

'Emily-May told me. It's been a long time, Mark.'

'Absolutely right,' said Drury. 'To be precise, seven years in July. The Deauville meeting or is that in August?'

There was no form of heating in the room but the windows were sealed tight. The sheets bore tea-stains and there was thick dust on the light bulb.

'Jesus, Mark,' Drury said impulsively.

Russell scratched himself vigorously. 'What are you now, some kind of social worker?'

Drury offered his cigar case but Russell refused. 'I owe you an apology, Mark. Don't make it tough for me. I should have let you take that money. The bank has taken over. The stud's gone, everything.'

Russell reached for the beer bottle, tipped it and wiped his mouth on the back of his hand. 'They nailed our Lord to the cross.'

Drury was patient. People could argue that he had it coming. 'I need your help, Mark.'

'Then you've come to the wrong place,' answered Russell. 'I couldn't get you into a two-bit poker game.'

'That's not the kind of help I'm talking about. Remember what Natie Crane used to say about con men?'

'Vividly,' said Russell. '"Those who don't die in the *pissoir* die in the poorhouse." A vulgar-mouthed fellow.'

Drury drew hard on his cigar. 'I don't intend to let that happen to me.'

Russell belched. 'Last time I heard of Natie he was living on a hundred thousand acres in New Mexico.'

'True,' said Drury, 'but he's the exception. He married a rich woman who straightaway realized that dying was a better bet than living with Natie. You and I are going to make that last big score.'

'Is that so?' Russell rolled over on his side and finished what was left in the beer bottle. 'I like a man who knows what he wants.'

'We're old and we're broke,' urged Drury. 'There's no place left for us to go except where we've been.'

'A philosopher, too,' Russell said sarcastically. 'It's great. You go around for years lifting your leg on people and suddenly there you are wagging your tail!'

Drury shrugged. 'OK, it's been nice talking to you, Mark. I know when I'm licked.'

Russell swung stumpy little legs off the bed. His long johns were in bad repair.

23

'What's your proposition? I need a stake to get out of here.'

Drury closed the door again. Mark had always played hard to get. 'We were the best in the business, right?'

'That was twenty-five years ago,' said Russell.

'They're still out there,' said Drury. 'Live wires with their hearts dripping with larceny.'

'Baldly stated,' said Russell scratching his chest. 'I've been in some financial distress. The problem's been Emily-May. If it hadn't been for her I'd have been out of Europe years ago.'

'If it hadn't been for Emily-May,' Drury said firmly, 'you'd have been shredded years ago. We're going on a boat ride and she's coming with us.'

Russell stopped with his trousers halfway up his legs. 'Now I know that you are losing your marbles.'

'Hear me out,' said Drury. 'Emily-May wants you picked up with your little nose wiped and returned as good as new. There's no room for half-measures. You're either in up to your ass or you're out.'

Russell fastened his belt under his bulging belly. 'It's always good to know your real friends.'

'You better believe it,' said Drury. He touched the canvas bag with the toe of his cordovan. 'Is this the sum total of your worldy possessions?'

'That's it,' said the little man. He stuffed some papers from a drawer into his pocket and grinned. 'Whatever is left behind may be given to the Society For the Relief of Distressed Gentlefolk.' He arranged the wisps of hair across his bald scalp.

Drury frowned as a cistern was flushed nearby. 'Downstairs,' said Russell.

'I'm out of touch,' said Drury. 'Do you know where we can get hold of a couple of books?'

'Sure,' said Russell. 'Pretty Sid the New Zealander's as good as the Passport Office.'

The name took Drury back. 'Is *he* still around?'

'Not in the same way,' said Russell. 'He took a fall in

Frankfurt and retired hurt. He's got a one-man printing outfit over in Fulham.'

'Printing outfit? I don't want that kind of book.'

'Whatever he's got is kosher. I used him last year. There's no one around any longer, none of the old mob. I had to team up with some clown out of Milan. So we find this South African in Milan and play the Rag to him, beat the guy for a million and a quarter lire. The Italian is holding the money, right? So what does the bastard do?'

'He takes off.'

Russell shook his head. 'He wants to buy this diamond ring for his girlfriend. So he lays three counterfeit hundred dollar bills on the jeweller.'

'A diamond for three hundred dollars?' asked Drury.

'Three hundred dollars and the rest in lire. The jeweller calls the law. Result, they put the arm on Mario and confiscate all the money he's carrying. It kinda disheartened me.'

'It would,' said Drury. 'There's something we have to straighten out before we start.'

'Like what?' Russell demanded, staring across the room.

'You were never too good at taking instructions,' said Drury.

Russell adopted a sply-legged stance. 'Continue.'

'Well, this is one time you're going to have to do exactly as you're told. There's too much at stake for one of your prima donna productions.'

'That's all?' asked Russell.

'That's all.'

'Right,' said Russell. 'Then let me tell you something. In all my life I never pulled less than my weight and you should know it. You don't have to worry about me.'

They eyed one another steadily and then shook hands, repairing a bond that had been stretched but not broken.

'Let's get out of here,' Drury said quietly. They walked downstairs to the lobby. Miss Hofmeister was still at the desk. She looked bewildered as Russell placed the key of his room in front of her.

'I'm leaving,' he announced.

She moved her head uncertainly, glancing from Russell to Drury who continued to smile.

'But I do not understand!'

'It's simple,' said Russell with a wave of the hand. 'Goodbye and *auf wiedersehen*.'

Her face flushed as the implications struck her. 'But this not possible. The manager will require to see you and he will not return before fife o'clock.' Emotion was playing havoc with her accent and syntax.

'Convey my very best wishes,' Russell said in a tone of deep sincerity. 'Kindly forward all mail in care of the American Ambassador in Tokyo.'

He stopped on the steps outside, looking across at the prostrate bums. He took a long deep breath. His bag had been left behind. His entire wealth was contained in the stained and mended Brooks Brothers blazer.

'I shouldn't have stomped that girl. Misery tends to make you want to give people a hard time.'

Drury shortened his stride to match his friend's. 'Age doesn't seem to have mellowed you. I hope you're going to behave yourself with Emily-May.'

Russell glanced sideways. 'You only see one side of that lady. She can be a downright menace. Did she tell you that she'd forced money on me?'

'She didn't exactly put it in those words, no.'

'She came to me, Phil,' Russell said earnestly. 'Sent me a four page registered letter. She said she'd just had a repeat on a script that she'd done. Why didn't I take the money and pay off my debts. There'd be no strings attached and so on.'

'Disgraceful,' said Drury, poker-faced.

'No strings, shit,' Russell said bitterly.

They crossed Praed Street and walked down the ramp into Paddington Station.

'You took the money, but you didn't pay your debts,' said Drury.

Russell's plump shoulders rose and fell. 'I took three to one to two grand and got beat on an objection for taking the second's ground. It taught me two things. First, never take money from a woman. Second, do anything you like with a horse except back it to win races. Either way you're in serious trouble.'

'I hear you don't gamble any more.'

Russell reached sideways, pulling Drury's jacket so that the two men faced one another. 'Did I ever tell you a lie?'

Drury released his coat from Russell's grasp. 'On an average, five times a day.'

Russell's face screwed up tight. 'This is incredible! A guy I've shared a toothbrush with!'

'That mistake was mine,' said Drury. 'State your case.'

'I haven't had a bet in eighteen months,' Russell said earnestly. 'I'm a reformed character.'

'That, as they say, will be the day,' said Drury and opened the door of a call box. He placed a coin ready in the slot and handed the phone to the other man. Russell was quickly out of the booth.

'He's there and he'll see us.'

They sat side by side in the taxi, Drury wondering how to ease his partner's notoriously delicate feelings when it came to money. Finally he pulled out his wallet and counted off four hundred pounds.

'This comes off the take with the rest of the nut. You'll need it for expenses.'

The cash disappeared as though by a conjuring trick. Russell grinned.

'I never forget a friend or a kick in the ass.'

The driver crossed the park and turned left halfway along Old Brompton Road where Drury paid him off. The coach houses in the mews had been turned into small business premises. There was a builders' office, a riding stable and at the far end Pretty Sid's sign screwed to the door. *Morton's Photographic and Printing Studio.* Russell pressed the bell. His clothes were shabby but the last half an hour had invested him with a definite swagger. A curtain moved in an upstairs window.

'He'll be down,' Russell said, nodding.

The door opened a fraction at first and then wider. It was twelve years since Russell had seen the man. The thick black hair was now grizzled, the once handsome features blurred. Pretty Sid was wearing overalls with a carpenter's pencil stuck through a buckle. He shut the door behind them hurriedly. Russell's hand wagged.

'You remember Phil Drury?'

Pretty Sid's nod of recognition was wary, as though remembering might cost him money. The other two men followed him into a large, well-lighted room with a wooden table covered with printing materials. A machine of some kind was clattering upstairs, causing the doors to vibrate in their frames. Pretty Sid lit a cigarette and closed one eye against the plume of rising smoke.

'What do you people want, I'm busy.'

'We want a couple of books,' said Drury, 'and you don't have to worry about the money.'

'I *always* worry about the money,' Pretty Sid answered. 'That's how I stay in business. Who needs the books, you or somebody else?'

'They're for us,' said Russell, 'and they have to be right.'

'All my stuff's right, friend!' Pretty Sid came off the wall, his expression offended. 'Expensive but right. I've got British, Canadian, Irish and American. Agewise I'd suggest the American and the Canadian. It's one thing less for me to have to alter.'

'Can we look at them?' asked Drury.

'Sure!' Pretty Sid climbed a flight of wooden stairs. It was a couple of minutes before he returned, holding up a couple of passports. 'These come from Rome but they're both stamped into this country. They're three hundred each, pictures included.'

Drury took a closer look at both passports. Neither carried a photograph.

'Are these things genuine?' Drury demanded. It was important to know.

Pretty Sid took the passports back. 'I already told you. They were hoisted in Rome. I just cleaned them up a bit. You could use them at a police convention. Do you want them or not?'

'How soon can you have them ready?'

The New Zealander thought. 'If I take your pictures now, a couple of hours.'

Drury counted out six hundred pounds. Pretty Sid looked from one man to the other.

'Which of you's the Canadian?'

'Me,' said Drury.

Russell looked down at the United States' passport. The occupation of the holder was described as 'farmer'.

'Can you take this out,' he asked, tapping the offending entry. 'Put in "priest S.J."'

'S.J?' Pretty Sid repeated.

'Society of Jesus. What's the name, "Jerzy Mitrega"? That has to be Polish. So a Polish priest, couldn't be better.' He rubbed his palms together.

'Right,' said the New Zealander. 'So that's Jerzy Mitrega, born Pittsburgh, Pennsylvania, June 2 1916 and Gordon Munro, born Walkerton, Ontario, August 11 1918.'

'Don't forget to put S.J. Father Jerzy Mitrega, S.J.' said Russell.

Pretty Sid shook his head. 'I can't take your picture looking like that. You look like a bum not a priest.'

'I'll be back first thing in the morning, dressed for the part,' said Russell. 'Deal with Phil.'

'You're the ones who have to get it on,' said the New Zealander. He assembled a Hasselblad on a tripod and seated Drury. He ran through half-a-dozen frames and straightened his back. 'That'll do you. I'll develop these tonight. If Russell gets here early in the morning, both books will ready by five in the evening.'

The two men hailed a taxi on King's Road that took them to the Danish-Lloyd offices in Lower Regent Street. Drury went in alone, leaving Russell in the cab. He handed the Paris voucher to a girl at the counter.

'I booked in Paris,' he said pleasantly. 'We weren't quite sure then who was going on the cruise. I have the names now. I'm Gordon Munro. The other passenger is Father Jerzy Mitrega.'

The girl showed the voucher to a man sitting behind at a desk. Drury scanned the posters on the wall. Danish-Lloyd specialized in cruises starting from the United States. The girl was back with the flight and cruise tickets properly inscribed. She gave them to Drury with a smile.

'That's Terminal Three on Friday, sir. Check-in time is ten twenty-five. Enjoy your holiday!'

Drury went outside to the cab. 'Carboy Street, Battersea.'

Russell made no move to open the folder that Drury had placed in his lap.

'Did I just hear you say Carboy Street?' he demanded.

'That's right.' Drury leaned back and stretched out his legs.

For the next ten minutes dissatisfaction leaked from Russell like syrup from a broken drum. From time to time he sighed and shook his head, blowing hard. Finally Drury could stand it no longer. He shut the glass partition between passenger and driver.

'What the hell's the matter with you? You sound like a pregnant rhinoceros!'

Russell turned an accusing eye. 'Why are you doing this to me?'

'Because this is the way Emily-May wants it. So do I. I want you where we can keep an eye on you.'

The cab slowed. The driver slid the glass back, nodding across at the pelican lights.

'I can't make a turn here. Will you people walk across?'

Drury pushed money at him and the two men used the pedestrian crossing.

'Now behave,' warned Drury. 'I know she tried to pay your debts, but be friendly.'

The door opened on the first ring. Emily-May stood there with a silk scarf setting off her Jaeger dress. She offered her cheek to Drury and looked Russell up and down.

'Good morrow, Sir Lancelot!'

Russell pushed by without answering. The other two followed him into the sitting room. The wastepaper basket was full of torn papers and the floor had been cleared of the litter. Emily-May's passport was lying on her desk together with an American Express envelope.

'Bridge Deck with a view port and stern,' she announced. 'Cabin one hundred and seventy-seven.'

Russell was leaning against the door, looking as though he was suffering from acute indigestion. Emily-May ignored him, addressing herself to Drury.

'Alison Bell's going to stay in the house while I'm away. She works for my literary agent.'

'That sounds good thinking,' said Drury. 'Meet a compatriot of yours, Gordon Munro out of Walkerton, Ontario. This here is Father Jerzy Mitrega of the Society of Jesus.'

'Hilarious!' Russell's tone of voice was sarcastic. 'What do you do for an encore, waltz?'

Emily-May considered him as though for the first time. 'But he looks so *well*, Phil,' she said, glancing at Drury. 'I mean the fuzzy outfit and all. I just can't find words for it.'

'That'll make history,' Russell said sourly.

Drury broke in hurriedly. 'Mark's going to stay here until we leave, if that's all right with you, Emily-May. This way I'll know he's out of mischief.'

The skin over her cheekbones reddened. 'He knows where his room is. I'll make only one condition. Those clothes will have to be thrown away.'

Russell stomped across the room and poured himself a

large scotch and water. He took it to the sofa and sat down glowering at Emily-May.

'He's not a man to be trifled with,' she said to Drury.

Russell wagged his head. 'It took me twenty-six years to break loose from you and he gets the cuffs back on me in less than two hours. Are the sheets clean on the bed?'

'How would you know the difference?' Emily-May's smile was ladylike.

'Such a bright abrasive dame. This is going to be beautiful.' Russell lifted his eyes to the ceiling.

'Go take a bath and get those filthy things off,' Emily-May said firmly.

He finished his drink deliberately and placed his empty glass on the mantel. He was not finished with them yet.

'I seem to be getting a lot of flak and we're not even started yet. I'll leave you with a thought. You people need me just as much as I need you.'

Seconds later they heard the sound of bath water running upstairs. Emily-May closed the door, an anxious look on her face.

'He hasn't been eating properly, I can tell.'

'Pure fantasy,' said Drury. 'The man's gross. He eats better than we do, you can bet on it. He's enjoying every minute of this, being the centre of attention. Give it a couple of days and the whole scheme will turn out to have been one of those brilliant Russell ideas.'

She turned from the drinks' cupboard. 'How about a glass of sherry?'

He nodded. She brought the two glasses to the sofa and sat down beside him.

'What did he say about me being along?'

He hunched his shoulders. 'I wouldn't say that he was exactly enamoured of the idea, but give it time.'

The house was strangely peaceful. Water splashing up in the bathroom, the nineteenth century patchwork, the feeling of *gemutlichkeit*.

Emily-May lit one of her cigarettes. She seemed less sure of herself now that Russell was out of the room.

32

'I wish I knew what to do with him, Phil.'

The sherry was too dry for his taste and he put the glass down. 'You'll find the right moves as the occasion arises. The main thing is that we found him and he's here.'

She was on her feet again, gesturing nervously with the hand that was holding the cigarette.

'I wish I could tell you how I feel about him.'

He brushed the suggestion aside. 'Don't even try. I have enough problems of my own.'

She stopped suddenly, halfway to the window, and swung around to face him. 'You think I'm crazy, right?'

He grinned. 'I'm sure of it. Look, honey, you don't have to worry about Mark. He's a survivor too, make no mistake about it. Take real good care of yourself.'

The door opened suddenly. Russell had on a well cut clerical suit with a roman collar. His skin was pink from the bath and he exuded an air of sanctity. He recharged his empty glass and considered them both.

'Is either of you for confession?' he asked sweetly.

Emily-May was the first to succumb, laughter bursting through the hand that covered her mouth. Drury grinned. The act was old but his partner's performace was always outstanding. Russell glanced at the clock.

'Tell you what, we'll hoist a couple of brews here and I'll take you folk out to supper.'

'I suppose that means that I'll need my purse.' Emily-May's face was under control again.

'No,' said Drury. 'He has money. But I'll have to take a rain-check. Judy's expecting me for supper. We'll meet here at noon tomorrow.'

Emily-May touched the back of her hair coquettisnly. Drury put his arms around her and drew her close.

'Just see that Captain Midnight keeps his nine o'clock date in the morning and don't listen to his blarney. There are things happening out there that would turn an innocent girl like you in her grave. Better you don't know about them.'

She found Russell with her free arm and pulled him so that she was standing between them.

'He'll behave,' she said fondly, looking down at his bald scalp.

'He'd better,' said Drury. He meant it in more ways than one.

It was getting on for seven o'clock and the street lamps were lit. Drury walked north to the river and then west along the Embankment. A couple of has-beens and a dizzy old broad were hardly the stuff to create panic at Interpol, yet he had an inner certainty that this was going to work. He boarded a Wimbledon train at South Kensington and joined the last of the homebound office workers. Once beyond Fulham, the train exchanged the tunnel for tracks high above the rooftops. Lights from windows splashed shabby backyards where starlings clustered on telephone wires. Drury gazed out through the dirty windows, his mouth set in its usual smile. But his mind was three thousand miles away.

Everything that people said, everything that he heard, suggested that the confidence trick was no longer considered an art form. The days of the old classical ploys, graded in their degrees of sophistication, had gone. So had the people who had practised them. He hadn't heard of a real score being made aboard ship in fifteen years. Sure, the cardsharps still turned a trick at bridge or poker and the odd jewel thief rode the more fashionable liners. But his kind of con man was finished. Or so they said.

He left the station and composed himself for the long uphill climb to his daughter's house. Her car was in the drive. He let himself in and found her in the sitting room, writing a letter, her legs tucked up under her. He saw its opening as he leaned over the sofa to kiss her. The letter was addressed to her bank manager.

Dear Mr Arnott,

I shall be away for at least a month as of next Friday. I am going on a Caribbean cruise with my father . . .

34

His tone betrayed none of his alarm. 'Have a good day, muddlehead?'

She looked up and smiled. 'A very good day.' She signed her letter and licked the gummed edge of the envelope. 'How about you?'

He shrugged, uncertain whether she knew that he had seen what she was writing.

'Not bad. I fixed the insurance business.'

He poured himself the drink he badly needed. There was a glass of Campari on the floor by her feet. She picked it up.

'I've got some news, too. But I'm not so sure that you're going to like it.'

'Try me,' he suggested. He stretched his leg carefully, feeling the threat of cramp. The good things in life go so quickly. At this hour he'd have been sitting in his study with the mares and foals snug in their boxes.

She sipped her drink, put her glass down, and came to kneel in front of him. She took his hands, obliging him to look at her.

'I'm coming on this cruise with you, Papa. I know you deserve a break, you've been through absolute hell. But I can't let you go alone. You need me. I managed to get one of the last few cabins. Three-one-five on A Deck.'

He smiled, too stunned to produce an argument even if he could have found one.

'You're crazy,' he said. 'Spending all that money unnecessarily. After all, being alone was the whole point of the trip.'

She tugged gently at his wrists, chiding him. 'You mean you don't want your daughter along? It isn't the moment for you to be alone. I was watching you at Orbec and I know about these things.'

He nodded, thinking of her own experience. She had come to him then.

'Look,' she went on. 'I'm not going to be your jailer, for God's sake. You do exactly as you please. And if you do feel like having someone to talk to, why I'll be there. After all, you and I are family.'

He stroked her cheek, smiling. 'Does it ever occur to you that you could be wasting your life?'

'No,' she said shortly. It was clear that she meant it.

'Well it should,' he reproved. 'You're twenty-nine years old and as pretty as a picture. You ought to be sharing your life with some nice guy instead of worrying about me.'

A faint flush appeared on her face. 'I'm thirty, not twenty-nine, and smart enough to know what I *don't* want. And I'd rather not talk about it any more. Guess what I've fixed for supper?'

He spread his hands. 'You're full of surprises.'

She strucked each item off on her fingers. 'Fresh salmon with that salad you like, the one with the charred bacon. Strawberries and cream and a bottle of blanc-de-blancs.

'The Savoy couldn't do better. All these virtues in one person, it's frightening.'

He walked into the kitchen with his arm around her waist and helped her set the table. He felt very close to her, close and helpless. It was too late now to pull out of the cruise. There were Russell and Emily-May to think about. They'd have to be people he had met for the very first time.

They ate by candle-light, talking little, content with one another's company. They killed two bottles of wine and Judy was a little tipsy by the time they had finished. She stared hard at the coffee percolator.

'You're my father. Nothing can ever change that.'

'A cryptic remark.' He moved the candlestick so that he could see her face.

She took her time answering. 'What I'm trying to say is that I want to help.'

He leaned forward across the table. 'You *do* help, honey. The trouble is that you worry unnecessarily.'

Her eyes were troubled. 'You really hate the idea, don't you – I mean me coming on the cruise with you?'

There was only one answer and he gave it with a smile.

'I'd hate it if you wanted to come and couldn't.' He looked at his watch and yawned. 'I'm bushed, sweetheart. Goodnight!'

Shafts of light pierced the cracks in the lined chintz curtains. Drury unwound his body, stretching and yawning in a cocoon of sheets and blankets. He had gone to sleep worrying about Judy and the worry was still there. He turned over on his back, composing a cable that would send his daughter scurrying back to Virginia. The trouble was there was no one to send it, no one but a distant cousin who had written off Drury long ago.

He reached for the curtain cord and flooded the room with pale sunlight. He found the floor with bare feet, breathed in deeply and scratched the small of his back. All he could hope for was to play things by ear and be lucky. He had one thing going for him. The conventions of the con-game required Russell to be a total stranger until the magical moment of his supposedly chance meeting with Drury. He would be keeping his distance in any case.

Judy was already up, the radio playing downstairs in the kitchen. He was tying the knot in his tie when a thought hit him like a sandbag. *He was Gordon Munro on the passenger list*! He completed the knot, resigned to telling yet another lie. He opened his window wide and went down to the kitchen. Judy was scrambling eggs at the stove. She offered a sweet smelling cheek. She had on a pair of tailored jeans and a sloppy joe sweater. Gold studs pierced her ears and she was wearing the aquamarine he had given her on her twenty-first birthday.

'Sleep well?' she asked.

He stared out into the garden, wondering how best to produce his latest excuse. A sound of frustration came from behind him.

'If only someone would make a pan that isn't a mess after scrambling eggs!'

He sat down, appreciative of the small touches. The

oranges had been segmented. Parsley sprigs decorated the butter. Her mother had taught Judy well.

'You're not hung over?' He spoke with his mouth full of orange.

'I never am on good wine.'

He bit into a piece of toast, nursing a suspect filling. 'I almost forgot. I'm down on the passenger list as Munro. There's been enough publicity about the sale of the stud and I'm sick of answering questions. Half the racing press is in the Caribbean at this time of the year.'

He'd have to be careful to go through customs apart from her, invent some excuse. Otherwise she'd see the Canadian passport.

She nodded. 'I wondered when I didn't see your name on the list.' They stared at one another for the space of seconds. 'More coffee?' she asked.

He pushed his cup across the table. 'What are your plans for today. I have to go into town again.'

She reached for a cigarette that he lit for her. 'I'll need some things for the cruise,' she said. 'Are we going to be sitting at the same table?'

'Of course,' he said and returned her Dupont lighter. 'You're not going to be playing nanny, are you?'

'What exactly is that supposed to mean?' Her eyes were wide.

He waved away the cigarette smoke. 'I'm thinking about your mother. Remember how she was whenever we went away? We were never allowed to be alone? She thought it bad for us.'

'I imagine I'll see enough of you at meals,' she said composedly.

'I have to go,' he said, standing. 'I'll be back around six.'

She started collecting the things from the breakfast table. 'I wish I knew what you're *really* up to.'

He stiffened, trying to maintain an appearance of innocence.

'Don't overdo it,' she said. 'Guilt's written all over your face. It's a woman, isn't it?'

He took the out as a trout does a mayfly. 'I'd rather not talk about it at the moment.'

Her eyes chased him to the door. 'Hold it! That's the *real* reason you're using another name on the cruise, isn't it? You're running away from some woman.'

It was weird that she was making things easy for him but every lie put him in deeper.

'I said I'd rather not talk about it,' he answered. 'I need time to think things out.'

She placed her hands on her hips. 'Aren't you going to tell me *anything* about her? Is she blonde, dark, fat or what?'

He shook his head, smiling but refusing to answer. She took his face in her hands and kissed him.

'Well, she'd better be nice whoever she is. I'm not having my father in the clutches of a harpy.'

It was noon when the taxi dropped Drury at the corner of Carboy Street. Emily-May opened the door, her face much softer than it had been on the previous day.

'He's in the sitting room.'

Russell was in his shirt-sleeves with his feet up on the sofa. The roman collar and his jacket were hanging on the back of a chair. A night's rest had done much for his appearance. The fat red face had been transformed into a semblance of benignity. He tossed a couple of passports at Drury.

'He threw in some stationery. I've typed a couple of letters.'

The letters were part of a con man's stock-in-trade to be left around for kibitzers to read. Drury held both passports to the light looking for a blemish that might trigger an immigration official's suspicion. The two photographs had the authentic self-conscious look and Pretty Sid had put in a couple of visas for good measure. Colombian for Drury's Canadian passport, Israeli for Russell. Russell winked.

'I must have been on a tour of the Holy Land.'

Emily-May came in carrying a tray and closed the door with her foot. 'I wonder how you dare,' she said to Russell and put coffee and biscuits on a table.

Drury dropped his bombshell. 'My daughter's coming on the cruise with us.'

Russell leaned back and closed his eyes. 'Beautiful! Just beautiful!'

The noises from the street were loud in the ensuing silence. 'There is no way out of it,' Drury explained. 'She's got it into her head that I'm involved with some woman. So she's made up her mind that I shouldn't be alone. There's nothing that I can do.'

Emily-May took the news in her stride. 'Has she ever seen Mark?'

Drury chased a biscuit with coffee. 'Never. Helen and I had been at the stud for some months when Judy was born. And she'd already married when Mark came to Deauville that time.' He felt uncomfortable at reviving a memory that did neither Russell nor him credit.

Russell was occupying the whole of the sofa, his eyes still fixed on the ceiling. Emily-May's face grew serious.

'I'd say that you're going to have to give an explanation to this young lady sooner or later.'

'I have different ideas,' said Drury. 'There's no reason why she should know a thing about my past or present. All it means is that Mark and I have to be a little more careful and that can't be bad.'

'Ah well, she's your daughter,' Emily-May said briskly and picked up the tray. The two men could hear her whistling out in the kitchen.

'I don't want to say this but I don't like the idea,' said Russell.

'You can always pull out.' Drury's tone was reasonable.

Russell swung his feet to the floor. 'You know I can't do that now, Phil. What I'm saying here is that you're making things difficult all round. First it was Emily-May, now it's your daughter.'

Drury's voice took on an unaccustomed edge. 'All you have to do is hustle your goddamn ass as you always did. There'll be money on that ship. Be the bird-dog you used to be and find it for me. I'll take care of the rest. What do you say?'

'What do I say?' Russell's fat face creased in a grin. 'I say trust in the Lord and keep your bowels open.'

'A typically elegant remark,' said Drury. 'What about these letters you've been writing?'

Russell passed the sheaf from the desk. He had used Emily-May's portable electric and the results were impressive. The envelopes bore recently cancelled foreign stamps and the letter-headings varied. Athabasca Copper Company, the Rand Mining Engineers Club, Business Security Inc. One imposing missive was handwritten on heavy blue paper embossed with the seal of the Colombian police. It testified to the good standing and reputation of Gordon Munro, Canadian citizen and quoted his passport number.

'I like the sealing-wax,' Drury said, returning the letters to Russell. 'It adds a note of authenticity.'

'You make an old man happy,' said Russell. 'God bless you!'

Drury rose as Emily-May came back into the room. 'I have to go, honey,' he said.

'OK,' she said, plumping out the cushions. Her eyes were bright. 'Necessity makes strange bedfellows.'

'So they say,' he replied. 'I'll see you people on Friday.'

TWO

The balcony overlooked coconut palms fringing the pool behind the hotel. Oiled coppertan bodies sprawled on the Bermuda grass, shielded from the fierce sun by thatch umbrellas. A Filipino waiter with a tray made his way treading delicately. Most of the charter boats in front of the hotel were missing from their slips, out trolling for marlin, tuna and dolphin or drift fishing. The owners of the boats still moored there were dozing on deck, reading or cutting up bait, all waiting for the chance customer who might take them out into the deep blue waters of the Gulf Stream.

Benjy stepped back from the balcony into the sitting room. A couple of inches over six feet, he had red hair and the clean-cut freckled good looks of a native Californian. He was wearing a flower-patterned shirt, linen pants and tasselled Gucci loafers.

'I guess I'd better go see this bum,' he said, stretching.

His brother was lying on the couch in his shorts. There was little physical resemblance between them. Sheldon was slim with the quick nervous movements of a small predatory animal. He lowered his magazine.

'Didn't Lansky say he's a lush?'

'Lansky said that he liked a drink.' Benjy thought back. He had exchanged the blinding light of Collins Avenue for the dim interior of the Maui-Paui Bar-and-Grill. The man waiting in the booth had the build of a hockey fullback gone to seed. His grey hair was worn unfashionably short.

'Ah, he's a schmock,' Benjy said carelessly. 'A schmock who wants to improve himself.'

Sheldon sat up a little straighter. 'How do you mean, "improve himself"?'

Benjy's smile revealed well-attended teeth. 'Look at it this way, Shel. OK, so he gets to dance with the passengers but the job pays zilch. Eight hundred dollars per. He wants to do better.'

Sheldon probed his ear delicately and inspected the result. 'That doesn't sound like a schmock to me.'

'He's originally from Grandsville, North Dakota,' said Benjy. 'He wants to go back there and raise goats.' He pulled the tab on a coke that was ice-cold and hurt his sinuses.

Sheldon spoke with the voice of authority. 'They don't raise goats in North *or* South Dakota. It's sheep.'

'OK, so it's sheep.' Benjy picked up the keys to the rented Chevvy, went into the bathroom and used his waterpick. He had no liking for Florida, mistrusting its climate and the fauna that it produced. He came back into the sitting room complaining.

'Every single thing you eat in this town tastes of this goddamn coconut.'

It was a week since they had flown into Miami. They had made their contact then driven down to Key Largo, reasoning that nobody there would know them.

Sheldon's tone was slightly argumentative. 'Tell me again why we need this guy.'

Benjy ran a comb through his red hair. He wasn't looking forward to the coming interview and the sight of Sheldon lying on the couch criticizing didn't help matters.

'We need him because he runs the radio room on the *Skagerrak*,' said Benjy over his shoulder.

Sheldon was unimpressed. 'He'll probably get howling drunk and cop all the wrong cables.'

Benjy turned away from the mirror. 'What are you, touting for Alcoholics Anonymous? Lansky found him. That's good enough for me.'

Sheldon yawned. 'I never did like these half-straight, half-crooked jokers. They're likely to pull the wrong half on you when it matters.'

'Get your beauty sleep,' said Benjy. 'I'll be as quick as I can.'

There was a breeze coming off the Atlantic but it was stifling inside the Chevvy. Benjy let down all the windows and got the air-conditioning going. The northbound causeway took him as far as Homestead where he turned east at the eighteen mile marker. This was a narrower causeway with just enough room for two cars to pass. It ran straight through a mangrove swamp, crossing what was virtually an island. It was muggy here, the sluggish water sheltered from the sun by ropes of Spanish moss. A board sunk into concrete bore the legend, *Jason's Motel Court and Alligator Farm.*

Benjy stopped the Chevvy outside an office constructed from cheap, weathered wood. Behind the office were half a dozen cabins built from the same unpainted planking. Alligators dozed on the mudbanks underneath the mangroves. Benjy closed his nose and averted his eyes as he crossed the crab grass. The rickety porch sagged beneath his weight. The office door was open. A ferret-faced youth inside was putting a new reel on a fishing rod. He was wearing cutdown jeans, basketball boots and a t-shirt with the emblem *I GOT TWO.* The office walls were thumbtacked with pictures of a pot-bellied man wrestling a dazed-looking alligator.

Benjy spoke from the doorway. 'Where can I find Mister Nielsen?'

The youth jerked his thumb. 'Out back.'

Benjy stepped forward purposefully. 'You can do better than that!'

The teenager looked at Benjy for the first time. 'What do you want, a guide dog? Number three.'

A seventy Dodge down on its springs was parked in front of the cabin. A television was playing inside. Benjy turned the doorhandle. The motel room was no better or worse than a million others across the country. Grey Tuftex carpet, a couple of Slumberwell beds, a Sears Roebuck calendar and a Gideon Bible. Nielsen stretched a long arm and switched off the television. On his feet he was as tall as Benjy and wore a blue short-sleeved shirt with faded jeans.

'Hi!' he said, lifting a hand. 'You want a drink?'

There was a dirty glass and a bottle of Jim Beam by the side of one of the beds. Nielsen's uniform was hanging from a rail in the showerstall.

'No,' said Benjy. 'Is it all right to talk?'

Nielsen waved a hand at the open door. 'There's only me and a pump salesman and he's out somewhere. These goddamn alligators drive you crazy at night, roaring and bellowing. They're worse than the mosquitoes.'

'Then why do you stay here?'

'Discreet,' said Nielsen. 'The kid's dumb and his father's always out whoring. And it's cheap. I thought about what you were saying.'

Benjy dusted off a chair and sat down. 'What's your answer?'

'I'm in,' said Nielsen. 'But it'll cost you.' Broken veins reddened his nose.

The chair creaked as Benjy leaned back. The stink of mud and alligators permeated the cabin, though a man who liked sheep probably wouldn't notice it.

'Let's get a couple of things straight before we talk money. You say you control everything that comes or goes from the radio room, right?'

'Every goddamn thing.' Nielsen's eyes were the colour of ice under a Northern sky and at the moment their expression was shifty. 'From a Mayday call from the bridge to Aunt Hannah's Get Well message.'

A mosquito droned out of the showerstall. Benjy suddenly wondered what he was doing holed-up with this hick.

'There's nobody else working with you?'

Nielsen slapped idly as the mosquito ghosted by. 'Not this trip there isn't. The kid got appendicitis last night. They couldn't find a replacement.'

'What about the records, the copies you keep or whatever?'

'That's me, too,' said Nielsen. 'Bionic Man, here, there and everywhere. Not only that I can pull the plug on any conversation and invent an excuse. That's why it's going to cost you.'

Benjy looked at him. The guy was as cool as a cucumber. 'Did Lanksy talk to you about money? I mean did he mention a figure?' Since Lansky rarely talked about anything but money it was likely.

'Yep,' Nielsen said briskly. 'But I wasn't listening. You're not dealing with some yokel here, pal. I'm offering a unique service. I can bury records, fake messages, anything you like but I got to be treated right. The tariff's simple. I get five hundred bucks for a fake call or cable, the same for a plug pulled or a preview.'

Benjy blinked sandy eyelashes. 'A preview.'

Nielsen sounded pleased with himself. 'That's right. A cable comes in for somebody else but you'd like to know what's inside. You get first peek. There is one more thing.'

'What's that?' asked Benjy.

'I get a grand up front and non-returnable. That's whether we do any business or not.'

'Shit,' said Benjy. 'I don't even know that we're going to use you.'

Nielsen widened his shoulders. 'Call it insurance.'

'How long you known Lansky?' Benjy demanded.

'A couple of months,' said Nielsen.

'He says you're from North Dakota?'

Nielsen seemed pleased. 'Right on and I'm going back there. I've been watching a thousand acres for years, up near the Canadian border. Its piss-poor land and cold enough to freeze the balls on a brass Buddha. You wouldn't think much of it.'

'I guess not,' Benjy agreed. That much he could be sure of. 'What kind of security is there on board the *Skager-rak*?'

'*Security?*' Nielsen's smile was without humour. 'Well, there's the purser. He's supposed to keep an eye open for any shenanigans. Then there's the master-at-arms. He sometimes does a little pussyfooting between decks. Anything big goes to the police at the next port of call.' He closed one of his cold blue eyes. 'I send the cable.'

Benjy reached for his wallet. It hurt to give this mother a grand, but he wasn't going to get anywhere without it. He counted out ten hundred-dollar bills. Nielsen stuffed them in his back pocket.

'I room down on D deck. I can always get to you in an emergency.'

Benjy's loafers were stained with crab grass. He glanced down at them with displeasure. 'Like I said, I can't be sure that we'll use you.'

'You will,' said Nielsen. 'You don't look the type to waste your money.'

Benjy rose to his feet. 'I'll see you on the boat, then.'

'Don't rush things,' warned Nielsen, coming to the door. 'Every damn fool on the cruise decides to make a call the moment they get on board ship. There are booths twenty yards away on the quay but that's no good to them.'

He peered outside, took a good look at the rented Chevvy, grinned and slammed the cabin door. The television set came on as Benjy started the motor.

He parked the car under the palms in front of the lodge. Some of the charter boats had returned and were moored in their slips. Men stripped down to their shorts were hosing blood and fish scales off the decks. Alley cats crouched possessively over scraps of guts and pungent debris. Benjy walked through gardens wet from the water-sprinklers, past the figures dozing on the porch and into the lobby. The place blazed with poinsettias. The clerk was reading the Hollywood race form. He looked up, giving Benjy the smile warranted by a hundred and fifty dollar a day suite. On the wall and behind the clerk were framed snapshots of the middle-aged Hemingway flanked by dying sharks.

'No messages, Mister Diamond.'

Benjy took his room-key. He liked using the names of precious stones as aliases. Sheldon would probably be out on the beach, breathing in and out or scouting the beach for what he called talent.

'We'll be checking out in the morning,' said Benjy. 'You can let me have the bill at breakfast.'

The clerk made a note. 'Sure thing, Mister Diamond.' He studied dentistry at nights at Miami University. He and Benjy had had long talks on the subjects of pyorrhoea and gingivitis.

It was considerably cooler up in the suite with the air-conditioner turned as high as it would go. The Puerto Rican maids worked in pairs and left early. The cushions in the sitting room had been shaken up, the beds turned back. Benjy took a shower and changed his clothes. No matter what the old-timers said, to make money you had to look money. The tan silk shirt and rust coloured trousers were from the Beverley Hills Boutique. He used the waterpick again, as always concerned with the state of his gums. The desk clerk had said that some diseases were hereditary. His father's last dental bill had been thirty-eight hundred dollars. Benjy winced at the thought of having his gums cut open and stitched back together again. It would be the old man's birthday in a few days' time. The cable of congratulation would be sent from Paris this year. Benjy and Sheldon rang the changes on countries. It might not convince their father but it sure as hell confused him.

Wolfie Field was going on seventy-three and living in the Carmel Valley. He had left Los Angeles when Benjy was still at the University of Southern California, he'd void Fields Electronics for eleven million dollars in cash and stock. Most of this, according to his sons, he sat on as though he was trying to hatch it. Benjy had done all the things he thought were required of him at school, acquiring two straight As and the knack of free-spending. Sheldon was heard from less, smarting under the spartan discipline of Dorchester Military Academy: an early interest in his own sex was responsible for the choice of school. A widower, Wolfie Field remembered his own Flatbush upbringing and moved to the Valley. Life at Oak Grove was good for three years. The ranch had its own airfield and a nine hole golf course. Benjy and Sheldon shared a three bedroom lodge where Benjy kept his Ferrari and polo ponies. Sheldon was madly in love with a golf pro at Pebble Beach and suffering. It was to end all too soon. A twenty-four-year-old refugee from East Berlin touched off a timebomb in the Field household. High-cheekboned with green eyes, Anneliese Grunelius caught Field senior's attention in the Carmel Health Food Restaurant. They were married six weeks later and Wolfie recovered his sex-drive. It took Anneliese two months to get rid of Benjy and Sheldon, badgering their father until he despatched them with a hundred thousand dollars apiece and an exhortation to do as he had done. They were aged twenty-four and nineteen respectively.

Picked up by a couple of visiting con men in Vegas, the brothers were fleeced of their patrimony in thirty-six hours. As pragmatists seeking further knowledge, they made no complaint to the police but hung around in Vegas hoping to find the men who had robbed them. By this time the con men had moved on to Europe. Benjy and Sheldon decided to analyze the tale that they had been told together with their reaction to it. The message was simple and clear. The only possible victims of the con game were people with larceny in their hearts. The brothers proceeded to apply this lesson to such purpose that two years saw them among the most successful teams of hustlers on the Coast. They worked only together, took few chances and preserved their clean records. Their relationship with their father and stepmother improved with time and distance. It pleased Benjy to invent and support a high-flying existence wherein he and Sheldon travelled the world, selling bulk meat to the Turkish Army, rolling-stock to Taiwan and dabbled in tankers laden with crude oil. Wolfie Field heard the news of their success with pride. They were good boys, hard workers, a credit. Good luck they deserved! Anneliese was less exuberant, content just as long as her stepchildren kept their distance.

Benjy carried Sheldon's body-magazine out onto the balcony. Purple and violet shadows softened the outlines of trees and buildings. The pool had been emptied and was now being cleaned. The night air was heavy with flower scent. White shirts glimmered under the palms as the waiters collected the empty glasses. It was too dark to read. Benjy swung around as he heard the sitting room door opened.

Sheldon's trousers and hair were wet. He was carrying his shirt.

'You're late,' Benjy said mildly.

'I met someone,' said Sheldon. He used the shower and emerged wearing a cowled white towelling robe and padded into the bedroom. Benjy followed.

'You're asking for trouble,' he said. 'One of these days you're going to land on some freak who'll carve his initials on you.'

'I can take care of myself.' Sheldon stepped into his shorts. 'So how did it go with Nielsen?'

Benjy moved his hand this way and that. 'I can't make up my mind about him.'

Sheldon grunted. His white shirt and blue slacks were from Mister Fish. He ran a comb through his hair.

'How much is it going to cost?'

'A grand. Up front and that's for openers.'

The full-length mirror lights came on and Sheldon eyed his reflection. 'What's he do for that, walk on water?'

'It's either that or nothing,' said Benjy.

'Screw him,' said Sheldon. 'We'll switch cruises.' He turned from the mirror, sleek and satisfied.

'We can't *do* that,' Benjy objected. 'Lanksy's our friend and he set the whole thing up.'

'Bullshit,' said Sheldon. 'Lansky ain't nobody's friend. Lansky's for hire. We do nothing, we need no protection.'

'That's a very naive statement,' said Benjy, looking at his brother. 'We're in Lansky territory.'

'So we move,' said Sheldon airily. 'I don't like the sound of this sheep-fancier.'

Benjy wrapped an arm around his younger brother's shoulders. 'Come on, baby, everything's going to be all right. Benjy'll keep an eagle eye on the fucker.'

'OK, OK!' The embrace had ruffled Sheldon's hair and he repaired the damage.

'I've asked for the bill,' said Benjy. 'We'll drop the car off at the Hertz office and take separate cabs to Dodge Island Terminal. You want to eat now or what?'

Sheldon nodded, blocking a yawn. They ate stone crabs, pepper steak and salad in the restaurant overlooking the bay, sharing the half-bottle of Mateus. They were in bed by ten. By the time moonlight touched the refilled pool, Benjy was snoring.

THREE

'*Canada?*' The cab driver glanced up in his rearview mirror. 'You got no race problem up there, right?'

'We keep that sort of thing under control,' Emily-May said firmly. The driver was black and friendly and she had the distinct impression that he was trying to make her. She found the idea at once ludicrous and flattering. He had extracted her nationality, marital status and reason for being in Miami during the four mile drive from Collins Avenue.

'England, you live in?' he continued. 'They got the problem there too. Did you see *Roots?*'

'I did not see *Roots*,' she replied. She used the Paco Rabanne spray on her throat and wrists. Her print dress was cool but the street temperature was ninety-six. It was a long time since she had been in this kind of heat.

Her answer kept the driver quiet as far as Biscayne Boulevard. He stopped his cab on Fortieth Street, reached back and opened the door for Emily-May. He jerked his head at the heavily curtained windows on the other side of the pavement, his black shiny face disapproving.

'This ain't no place for a lady.'

'I'll survive,' she said smiling, and gave him ten dollars.

A masked androgynous figure decorated the window, one of its hands holding a card that read *Chez Coquette*. Emily-May stepped through the door into twilight. It was some time before her eyesight adjusted. She was in a rectangular room and facing a maplewood bar backed by a blue-glass mirror. The walls were papered with aluminium foil with a tobacco plant motif. Black glass divided the booths and the tables were made of plastic and chrome. A heavy blank-faced woman in a lurex top was playing Noël Coward at the piano, chewing gum with her eyes fixed on the ceiling.

Emily-May took a few steps forward, peering round in search of Russell. Most of the booths were occupied by men. The blond barman stiffened appreciably as Emily-May approached. The man he was talking to turned in sympathy. Both wore a look of surprise. Emily-May spotted Russell alone in a corner booth. She bore down on him. As she did so, the pianist went into the beginning of *Jealousy*, her eyes still fixed on the ceiling. Emily-May sank into the seat beside Russell, her voice shaking with fury.

'How *dare* you, goddamnit? How dare you bring me into a place like this? Just what do you think you are doing?'

The decor offended her more than the clientele. Russell was wearing a new tropical-weight clerical suit and had acquired a panama hat. He frowned into his old-fashioned.

'I had to see you, Emily-May.'

She looked at him hard but he refused to meet her gaze. His new smile was an expression of forbearance and it maddened her.

'See me – what for?' she demanded.

He groped along the bench until his hand touched her knee. 'You looked gorgeous coming through the door.'

She removed his hand brusquely. 'Your linguistic powers are hardly legendary, but is that really the best you can do? Why have you brought me here?'

'I told you, I wanted to see you.'

'God damn you, Mark Russell,' she said feelingly. 'I wonder why I bother with you. A few dollars in your pocket and you're an arrogant oaf. I get a message to meet you in a bar that even a hard nosed hack turns up his nose at. Do you realize that there are twelve couples in the place and I'm the only woman?'

'I didn't know,' he said defensively. 'I picked the name

from the phone book. You've taken me to a helluva lot worse places. Why is it that no matter what I try to do, you stomp me with both feet?'

'Why is it?' she repeated. The truth was complex and only peripherally connected with what was happening now. The essence was that this small fat man was the husband and child she neither wanted nor needed. She just happened to love him.

She shook her head. 'You don't know it, Mark, but you've got a deep seated desire to revenge yourself on me. That's our big problem. Nothing's enough for you but then anything is too much. You're an unhappy little man.'

He shook his head, his voice sincere. 'You're crazy. I'm not unhappy. You just don't understand me. You never have.'

'I'll give you that one,' she said at last. 'Now are you going to tell me why I'm here?'

'Phil asked me to see you about his daughter.' His face was unabashed.

The pianist was playing *Stardust*, her eyes still fixed on the ceiling. Emily-May lit a cigarette.

'His *daughter?*'

'That's right. Phil wants you to get her off his back. Pick her up and make a friend of her. She's been hanging onto his hand ever since we left London.'

It was likely. Emily-May had seen them together on the plane, in the bus from Miami International, at breakfast that morning.

She took a sip from Russell's glass. 'How come he asked you and not me?'

For a second his face wore the endearing expression of a puppy. 'He knew I wanted to see you.'

Emily-May relented, glancing around. 'It could have been worse, I guess. But not much.'

His hand had found her knee again. This time she allowed it to stay.

'Phil can't move as things are,' he said. 'And he can't

come right out and tell her to back off. You've got to do something about her.'

Emily-May stubbed her cigarette out. 'That's easier said than done from the look of her.'

'You're cute,' said Russell. 'I'd like to go to bed with you right now.'

She freed her knee from his grasp. 'That does it. I'm leaving.'

'Don't go yet,' he pleaded. 'Look, it could be weeks before we're together again. I'll tell you what, come to my room after supper. I'll leave the door unlocked. Eight-two-five up on the eighth floor.'

There was no way in which he could have been overheard but Emily-May felt the blood rising on her bosom and neck.

'Come to your room? Just what do you take me for?'

He tried to take her hand and failed. 'A lovely lady who should be living life instead of writing books about it.'

'Well shucks,' she said sarcastically. 'That almost brings tears to my eyes.'

The men at the bar were staring in their direction and she saw the implications clearly. A priest, a woman of a certain age, a rendezvous in a homosexual bar. She picked her bag and sunglasses from the table.

'I'm leaving right this minute. And don't you dare to come after me, you lecherous old goat.' She rose, smiling sweetly. 'Goodbye, Father, it was great seeing you again.'

Intolerable heat lifted off the pavement outside. There was no shade at all. She flagged down a cab at the end of the causeway and told the driver to take her to the hotel. The yachts were out, water-skiers defying gravity. She leaned back, thinking about the man she had just left. The events of the last three days had hardened Russell's sense of his own importance. The gambling bug may have been cured but little else seemed to have changed.

Her room faced Collins and overlooked the ocean. She

double-locked and bolted the door and lay down on the bed in her shift. It was too bright to sleep and she read. It was just after seven when she changed into a long dress and put on her garnets. She had done all her shopping at Liberty's, ignoring the advice of the sales girls. The result, she felt, justified her decision. The fine, pink-tinged linen softened the outlines of her body.

The Grenadier Bar was empty. She tried the bar on the other side of the lobby. A harpist was playing soft jazz. Some of the people she recognized. They had been on the plane and she assumed that they were joining the cruise. Phil Drury's daughter was sitting in front of a glass tank filled with tropical fish. Emily-May bought herself a glass of chilled sherry and carried it across. She was careful not to anticipate the younger woman's decision.

'Do you mind if I join you, my dear?'

Judy's voice and manner offered common courtesy. 'By all means do!' She removed the beaded evening bag from the top of the table. She bore little resemblance to her father with a tipped nose, blonde hair and dark blue eyes. She was wearing an ivory coloured silk dress and an amethyst ring.

Emily-May sat with her back to the fish tank. 'Damn things make me nervous,' she volunteered. 'I keep seeing faces that I recognize.'

'I know what you mean.' Judy's smile was polite.

Emily-May tasted her sherry and made a face. 'Like vinegar! I noticed you on the plane coming over from London. You were with an older man, very distinguished looking. Is that your husband?'

'My father.'

'And are you on the *Skagerrak* too?'

Judy put her glass down slowly. Something about the way she did it prompted Emily-May to break in. 'You'll have to forgive me, my dear. I'm just a nosey old spinster.'

'I don't believe that for one minute,' said Judy, shaking

her head. Hostility had faded from her face. The tack had clearly been the right one. 'That was my father.'

'Have you travelled Danish-Lloyd before?'

'No,' said Judy. 'As a matter of fact it's my first cruise. My father's been through a pretty rough time and I wanted to be with him.'

'I know how it is,' Emily-May said with quick sympathy. 'And do you live in London?'

There was a hint of indecision before Judy replied. 'I have a house in Wimbledon. My father was living in France but he's staying with me for a while.'

Emily-May reached across and touched the other woman's hand. 'I'm Emily-May Hurran and I'm Canadian as you might have guessed. I live in London too and it's *my* first cruise! I'm not so sure that I'm going to enjoy it.' Her nod indicated a couple of men at the bar who were plainly drunk.

'I'm Judy Ashe. Divorced. I have to go now. I expect we'll meet again.'

Judy was on her feet, looking across the room. Drury was standing in the entrance, handsome in his black dinner jacket as opposed to the white and tartan tuxedos.

Emily-May watched the couple across the lobby. Drury tucked his daughter's arm under his own. The table he had booked was in an alcove of the Lafayette Restaurant, a long room with white paint and gilt mirrors and a view of the empty beach. The moon was up, silvering the sea.

Drury ordered a bottle of Krug '71 and shifted the candle the better to see his daughter. She put her head on one side. 'Are we celebrating something?'

He nodded. 'It's cold and grey in London and I'm here entertaining my beautiful daughter.'

Age had nothing to do with it and it wasn't just looks. He was still the most interesting man in the room. She toyed with the stem of her glass, looking at him lovingly. He was a hard man to help, a giver rather than a taker. The thought had been in her mind for weeks but she voiced it now impulsively.

'Why don't we set up home together – I mean permanently? I could sell up in London and we could move to New Mexico.'

He made a face. 'Pottery, poetry readings, burlap dresses and all that goddamn desert, hell no!'

Emily-May was crossing the room, towering over a Cuban waiter. She waved over at Judy who responded.

'Who's your friend?' asked Drury.

She shrugged. 'She's on the cruise, a Canadian. Nosey, but nice, if you know what I mean. She's probably lonely. You didn't answer my question, about living together.'

'A thing like that needs thinking about,' he said light-heartedly.

'That's right,' she agreed. 'And now is a good time to do it. We could have our own quarters, be entirely independent of one another. Forget New Mexico, what about Washington or Oregon?'

He sighed. 'I guess I've lived too long in Europe, honey.'

The arrival of the trolley put a temporary halt to the conversation. The waiter raised the cover of the dish, his helper hovering anxiously. The lobster meat had been arranged in the shape of a crown and decorated with tomatoes baked in butter and paprika. The sieved lobster coral was crushed with pimento. Judy looked down at her plate and drew a deep breath.

Drury raised his glass. 'Santé!'

'*A la tienne*!' They drank, their eyes fixed on one another.

Drury ran his tongue along his lower lip. 'Excellent!'

'OK,' said Judy. 'We won't talk about it any more. I mean living together.'

He held up a finger, smiling. 'It's a question of *where*, not if. I'm glad you've made friends.' He nodded across at Emily-May who was eating alone.

Judy used the crackers on a lobster claw. 'That's not very subtle, but I take your point. Don't worry about me, Papa. I'll find plenty to do.'

They drank their coffee outside. Frogs were croaking and the night shimmered with fireflies. Drury sipped his Courvoisier.

'This is the best part of the day. I can't take this kind of heat any more.'

Judy's face was out of the light. 'I guess you still want horses?'

It was an innocent question yet it cut to the heart of the matter.

'Yes,' he said quietly. 'I still want horses.'

'Another stud?'

'Another stud,' he agreed.

'But you don't have the money?'

'That's right, too.' He thought aloud. 'But with any sort of luck I will have.'

His daughter stared hard at him. 'And where would you get that sort of money? Is that where this woman comes in – is she rich?'

He closed his right eye. 'I'm not telling.'

She leaned forward as though unwilling to miss the slightest change of expression on her father's face.

'But I'm the one person that you *should* tell!'

'Don't be contentious,' he said. 'All will be known in good time. Your father doesn't give up all that easily.'

She put out her cigarette, shaking her head. 'When the good Lord chose your vocabulary he left out the word "modesty".'

FOUR

Russell opened his eyes cautiously. He was lying on his bed wearing no more than his underpants. It was four o'clock in the afternoon and he had eaten too many baked oysters for lunch. They were a day out of Miami, steaming south-south-east at twenty-two knots an hour. They had left Eleuthera behind just after noon.

He pulled himself up with an effort and gently massaged his stomach. He went to the window, gaping. The ocean looked like rippled glass. He turned away hurriedly, nauseated by the sudden memory of the New Yorker at lunch who had halted in the middle of some interminable story to rush from the table ashen faced, cheeks bulging and holding his napkin to his mouth. He had not been heard from again.

Russell unlocked a drawer and poured himself a stiff jolt of Armagnac. He sat down, grateful for its fire in his stomach. The movement of the stabilized ship was gentle and he had never been seasick but right now he was close to it. The telephone rang. He reached across the six channel radio and picked up the receiver.

'Hello?'

'Father Mitrega?' The voice was unfamiliar.

Russell slipped in his top denture. 'Speaking.'

The voice continued with a sort of oily familiarity. 'This is Elwood Voitek, your purser, Father. Remember? We met at lunch. I hope I haven't disturbed you.'

'I was reading my office,' said Russell and belched without sound. He wondered what the hell the purser could want him for.

'I was wondering if we could have a little talk, Father,' said Voitek.

Russell stood up, his paunch protruding over the elastic of his shorts.

'A little talk?' he repeated, playing for time.

'A personal matter – well not really *personal* as much as spiritual. Do you get my meaning, Father?'

Jesus God, thought Russell, not confession! He had been posing as a priest for twenty-five years on and off, but he could still be caught offguard. A certain amount of testiness crept into his voice.

'What exactly are you talking about, Mister Voitek?'

'I'd sooner discuss it in my office, Father, if you could spare the time.'

'I'll be there in a few minutes,' said Russell. He put the phone down and looked at it speculatively. Goddamn this sonofabitch, what *was* all this? A thought occurred as he was pulling on his pants. The purser was supposed to be the captain's ears and eyes, the officer who had most contact with the passengers. Russell opened the locked drawer again, pulled out the Mitrega passport and took another look at it. He had already passed through three immigration checks, Heathrow, Miami International and the Dodge Island Terminal. But law-enforcement officers had ways of marking a passport for the edification of their colleagues elsewhere. It could be a faint pencil-tick, a date stamp set at an odd angle, a signal that the holder of the passport might warrant further investigation.

Russell held each page to the light but saw nothing suspicious. He locked the passport back in the drawer and dressed in his new lightweight clericals. The collars he had bought in Miami were soft and did not chafe the neck. He arranged his wisps of hair, swallowed a couple of mints and picked up his *Life Of Saint Ignatius Loyola*. The signs downstairs led him past the bank and beauty parlour, the radio room and the bureau. The purser's door was marked *Private*. Russell tapped and entered. The desk and metal files were attached to the floor, the steel-grey walls

61

undecorated. Voitek rose, hawk-nosed and dark haired, his tropical whites showing off his deep tan. His eyes were deep set.

'Thanks for coming, Father.'

He fussed Russell into a chair and sat down behind his desk. Russell was less than reassured by the purser's appearance.

'What can I do for you?' he asked, folding his hands across his stomach. He sounded about as forthcoming as a loan-shark approached by some no-hoper.

Voitek's manner was almost conspiratorial. 'You're a Jesuit, right, Father?'

'That's what it says on my passport,' Russell said lightly. There was no sign of danger that he could see, no papers out on the desk. The only thing in evidence was an old-fashioned carpet bag on the floor near Voitek's feet.

The purser's manner changed to a sort of croaking geniality. 'I was at a Jesuit school, St Joseph's in Tampa. You can imagine how I felt when I saw your name on the passenger list.'

Russell played it safe with a nod. Voitek went on. 'Will you believe it when I tell you that this is my seventh tour of duty aboard the *Skagerrak* and this is the first time we've had a priest on the ship. I'm not going to beat about the bush, Father. We'd like you to say mass for us.'

Russell assumed an expression of benevolent doubt with extreme difficulty.

'Well now . . .' he started.

Voitek had the bit between his teeth. 'I've already run a head count. We've got over a hundred Catholics in the crew. I'd guess more among the passengers. Captain Bishop conducts a non-denominational service on Sundays but that's not good enough. We want our own service, Father.'

Russell belched involuntarily, wishing that he'd hit himself with another belt of the Armagnac. 'It's not quite as easy as you think.'

Voitek grinned like a wolf. 'Let me take a guess – you're still dancing the old-fashioned way, right, Father?'

Russell opened his mouth, but no words came out. Voitek's face became even more vulpine. 'If you're still saying the Latin mass you're in the right ball park, Father.'

'It's not that!' Russell's voice was suddenly strident. 'I'm supposed to be convalescing after a heart attack.'

'A short service,' said Voitek. 'No excitement. We'll take real good care of you.'

Russell groped desperately. 'There's the matter of vestments and vessels. We don't carry these things around with us, you know.' He hoped that the thing flowed with a ring of conviction.

'I knew you were going to say that!' Voitek grinned. 'I've got this cousin who's a priest in Saint Petersburg. I drove down there just as soon as I saw your name on the passenger list. Francis lent me the works. Take a look at this!'

He opened the carpet bag, revealing a bottle of sacramental wine wrapped in a complete set of vestments. There was a small brass crucifix and a monstrance. Voitek's voice came to Russell through the noise of the marksmen outside shooting clay pigeons.

'Now come on, what do you say, Father?'

Russell could hear the whirr of the air-conditioning but it was suddenly very hot in the office. His smile was sickly. Creeping Jesus, he thought, it must be forty-six years since he last served mass. He fixed his eyes on the crucifix, licking his lips.

'When were you thinking of?'

'Tomorrow, Father. We can use the theatre just as soon as the Captain is through. Leave everything to me. There's no need for you to worry.'

Russell nodded wordlessly. He had to sit down and do some rapid thinking. He rose.

'You're forgetting your bag,' smiled Voitek.

Russell walked along the corridor carefully, the smile

still pasted on his face, adjusting to the slight roll of the ship. He unlocked his cabin and closed the door behind him. Then he sat in one of the armchairs, the carpet bag between his feet. After a while he bent down and opened it. The sacramental wine bore the label *Approved by the Diocese of Los Angeles. Pure Grape Product*. Mother of Jumping Jesus! He shook his head and picked up the missal. He opened the soft leather covers and read. It had been printed in 1937 and the text was in two languages. The mass read by the priest and the responses were in Latin, the instructions to the laity in English. He mouthed a few of the Latin phrases then threw the missal at the bed. He took a good look at himself in the mirror and shook his head. He was never going to be able to hold this together, never in a million years. His masquerade as a priest had put him in some spots in the past but this was something else. He'd have to fake a fit or something.

He lit a cigarette with a shaky hand and called Drury's cabin. There was no answer. Russell kept trying, becoming a little more desperate with each failure. It was well after six before the call was finally answered.

'Gordon Munro!'

His partner's easy confidence only made matters worse. 'You'd better get over here fast,' said Russell. 'I'm in my room.'

He unfastened the door and sat watching it. An age seemed to elapse before it was opened. Drury came in exuding conservative prosperity in his dinner jacket and cummerbund. His face sobered as he looked at his partner.

'What's wrong with you?' he demanded.

There was a certain amount of satisfaction in sharing the load. 'We're a mile up shit creek and no paddle,' said Russell. 'They've asked me to say mass.'

Drury sat on the edge of the bed, listening as Russell explained. It was a moment before he showed any reaction then he started to laugh, the veins in his neck contorted.

Russell waited, stiff with indignation, until Drury was able to control himself.

'Enjoy yourself,' Russell said grimly.

Drury wiped his eyes with his handkerchief. 'I'm sorry.' He bent down and peered into the carpet bag. Then he looked up. 'You're going to have to go through with this, Mark. We don't have an alternative.'

'*We* don't?' repeated Russell, his face dangerously red.

Drury spread his hands. 'You're the priest. Look at it from another point of view. This could be a godsend. People are going to be talking about that fine little father who said mass for the faithful.'

'Horseshit!' said Russell who could see the doors of the trap closing on him. 'I can always take to my bed, *that's* an alternative.'

'Not a very good one,' said Drury. 'They'll be in here reading prayers over you. You'd have to spend the entire cruise lying on your back and I need you out there hustling.'

The ships' engines hummed in the distance. The sun was sinking and passengers walking outside threw their shadows across the gauze window curtains.

Russell sank his head in his hands, deeply despondent. 'I can't do it, Phil. It's more than forty years since I did any of that shit.'

'You can do it,' Drury said confidently. 'In the first place people think you're a priest. That puts two strikes against them. You can be boring, forgetful, drunk at a push, but for them you'll always be the priest.'

Russell leaped at the phone as it rang. It was Voitek. 'I've talked with the Captain, Father. He'll be glad for us to use the theatre at eleven o'clock. I'll have the notices put out.'

Russell replaced the receiver. 'That does it! That asshole's fixed things for eleven o'clock.'

Drury glanced at his watch. 'We'll work something out.'

Russell shook his head despondently. 'What the hell am I going to do, Phil?'

'Rehearse.' Drury leaned forward, his mellow voice persuasive. 'We'll rehearse the act together.'

Russell's face took on the expression of a nudist who has sat on a hornets' nest.

'*Rehearse*? What the hell do you mean, rehearse? What do you think this is, some song-and-dance act?'

Drury stopped him with an uplifted hand. He leafed through the missal and read a few lines from the *Introit*.

'Come on, Mark, we'll give it twenty minutes.'

He arranged the crucifix on the dressing table and dropped the chasuble over Russell's head.

'Cameras, action, go!' he said.

Russell pulled himself up, smiling feebly as if in a dream. 'I'm not going to like this, Phil.'

Russell arranged the silk stole on his shoulders. Drury stuck the missal in his partner's hand. 'Grit your teeth and think of Acapulco.'

Russell's eyes sought the printed pages, stumbling through unfamiliar phrases and language until he gained confidence. He checked the mirror from time to time for signs of levity from behind. But Drury was leaning forward in prayerful attitude, one hand covering his eyes. By the time Russell reached the *Miserere* he was going well, his memory recreating pictures and guiding his brain. He took a shot at a blessing and made a couple of shaky genuflections. Then he turned.

'Shit, that's it! I need a drink.'

'Not bad,' said Drury, smoothing his hair in the glass. 'I'm having a drink with your lady and Judy. We'll get another rehearsal in later.'

FIVE

It was ninety-eight degrees on the deck outside. The pretty girl in blue and white uniform was trying to deal with difficult passengers at the Bureau counter. The bank was closed and people wanted to cash cheques, others had queries about their cabins. Sheldon Field summoned the little-boy-lost look that usually served him well.

'I'm the world's worst when it comes to remembering names. You won't believe this but I even forget my own brother-in-law's though that's no bad deal.' He winked.

It was the third day out and the girl had been on duty since nine o'clock that morning. Beads of sweat showed on her upper lip and her poise was slipping.

'I don't really see how I can help you,' she said to Sheldon. 'Not unless you can remember your friend's name.'

Sheldon was supposed to be tracing a mythical Jake, patronymic unknown, a man he had met in New York and who was on the cruise. Sheldon leaned across the counter persuasively.

'If I could take a peek at the passenger list ... '

'You'll have to excuse me, sir,' she said firmly, turning back to the couple with the noise problem. Their cabin was over the disco and they wanted to change it.

Sheldon was a veteran at this sort of encounter. 'Maybe I should speak to somebody else about it,' he suggested. 'I mean, if I could see the list I might get inspired. Who's in charge around here?'

The girl closed her eyes briefly, took a folder from her desk and all but slapped it down in front of Sheldon. He turned the pages slowly, affecting an interest in the rows of names. The couple with the noise problem were keeping the girl busy. The man was a lawyer, he announced, and he had no intention of paying a supplement in order to have a decent night's rest. There were such things as cruise contracts. Sheldon had already found the listing he wanted. The occupant of room one-zero-one was a Mister Gordon Munro.

He closed the folder, signifying defeat as he caught the girl's eye. She managed a weary smile. Sheldon hurried up the stairway to the Bridge Deck. Gordon Munro. He had seen the guy with a good-looking chick on a few occasions, sometimes with an older woman, in the bars and watching the clay pigeon shooting. Sheldon opened the door to his brother's cabin. Benjy was lying on the bed, reading. The radio was tuned to a station playing Hoagy Carmichael.

Sheldon lowered the volume. 'The guy's name is Munro. Gordon Munro.' He had followed the man to his cabin after lunch.

Benjy put his magazine down. 'It's got a good ring to it. Gordon Munro. What about the girl?'

Sheldon shook his head. 'If she's his wife they're not sleeping together. He's alone. And something else, that cabin's setting him back the best part of nine grand.'

'I like it,' Benjy said happily. 'Maybe the girl is a friend.'

'That kind of friend he'd be sleeping with,' said Sheldon.

'Why don't you think of something else besides sex?' Benjy reproved. 'She could be his daughter.'

'Whatever,' Sheldon said indifferently. 'Now the other one, she *is* a friend.'

Benjy poured them both a coke. 'All those cabins on the Sun Deck are graded AA. There are only sixteen of them.'

'The most expensive on the boat,' said Sheldon significantly.

'I hear sweet music,' said Benjy. Three days at sea had

burnished his Californian tan. He swung bare freckled legs to the floor and slipped his feet into a pair of *huaraches*. He turned the volume of the radio up again and snapped his fingers to the beat of the music. 'I'm getting the right vibes from this turkey.'

Sheldon killed the radio entirely. 'You want a trip down memory lane, do it when you're alone.'

Benjy's face was good-natured. 'Mister Munro gives me a good feeling, Sheldon. The something indefinable that only Uncle Benjy senses.'

'You're talking crap.' Sheldon dropped his coke can in the basket. 'So what do we do about him?'

'We play it by ear,' said Benjy.

'Play it by ear,' Sheldon said again. 'Now what in hell is that supposed to mean?'

Benjy went to the window. The dolphins astern were leaping high out of the water, silver and black in the sunshine. He turned.

'See how things go. If the right moment comes along tonight, why then take a crack at him. If not, some other night. We've got plenty of time to beat the sucker.'

'Right,' said Sheldon. 'And if it isn't him it'll be somebody else.'

'That, too, is valid,' said Benjy. 'Our life is just about to take a turn for the better. Just one thing, Shel. No weird dressing or make-up, OK?'

'Up yours!' Sheldon retorted and slammed the door. His cabin was on the other side of the boat. Gulls swooped low past the portholes chasing the scraps that someone below was throwing to them. Sheldon showered and put on a grey linen suit and a lilac shirt worn without a tie and open at the neck. The hell with Benjy, indeed. Sheldon's image was of a slightly bohemian whizz kid, one of the new breed of Hollywood agents. He dabbed himself with Etienne Aigner and took a close look at his temples. His hair was definitely thinning in spite of the Pallas Clinic. Five hundred dollars for six sessions. Electrical shocks applied by a dyke in a nylon surgical smock. A rip-off.

He unlocked a bag and took out a glossy-paged magazine assembled by a printer in downtown Los Angeles. Paper and artwork were excellent, the articles culled from all over. There was something there for everyone. A review in depth of steel production in Taiwan, a piece on films made for television, a report on British control of world insurance. The name of the magazine was *High Finance*. He opened it at the centre spread on a half-tone picture of Benjy over an article with a London byline.

INDEPENDENT REMAINS AN ENIGMA

Chester Black flew out from Heathrow last week refusing to confirm or deny rumours that his prospecting company had discovered extensive new oilfields on block 18/4b in the North Sea. A spokesman for Battlegrey Inc stated in Paris last night that it was not seeking public money at this time or in the foreseeable future. Battlegrey stock is held entirely by Mr Black's family and friends.

Sheldon tucked the magazine under his arm. It was almost seven o'clock. He heard the lift stop and people coming along the corridor. Beyond the passdoor outside Sheldon's cabin were the wheelhouse and executive officers' quarters. The older woman he had seen with Munro was on the same deck. He and Benjy would have to be careful.

The Promenade Deck was devoted to the ease and entertainment of the passengers. Here were the theatre, the outdoor swimming-pool, the casino and disco. A five-piece mariachi band was playing in the Central Lounge. Sheldon checked the Four Winds Bar and the Lido. There was no one in either. He walked forward to the glass enclosed observation cabin. There were two of them. Spray covered the heavy plate glass, causing the colours of sun and sea to run. He waited a quarter of an hour then strolled aft. He could see the Lido Terrace from the gallery. Gordon Munro was down there, sitting alone at the bar. Sheldon picked up the nearest phone and called Benjy's room. He waited, hidden behind a pillar, until he saw his brother's red head then followed him into the bar. Benjy had taken the stool next to Munro. The only other people apart from the barman were a honeymooning couple who had chosen a table as far away as they could. The terrace doors were open to the deck. The shifting surface of the pool was touched with moonlight. Strings of coloured lights traced the graceful lines of the ship.

Sheldon took the stool on the other side of Munro. He now had a brother each side of him. Sheldon ordered a drink, catching sight of Munro's face in the glass. He smiled but there was no response. Sheldon continued to look into the glass, frowning at his brother's reflection. He made a token movement, as if to open the magazine in front of him, then shrugged. Benjy finished his drink, signed the voucher and nodded to the barman. Sheldon leaned forward confidentially, claiming the barman's attention. He jerked his head after Benjy's well tailored shoulders.

'Isn't that Chester Black?'

The Puerto Rican shrugged then and, eager to be of service, glanced down at the voucher.

'Ees Meester Black, yess!'

Sheldon turned, involving the distinguished-looking stranger in conversation. 'Isn't that the damnedest thing? I was reading about the guy only ten minutes ago.'

He opened the magazine and passed it along the bar. Munro donned a pair of reading spectacles and read the centre spread through. He put his spectacles back in a crocodile case and smiled politely.

'Seems as though he has a good reason to take a cruise.'

'I'd like to have the same reason,' said Sheldon and put out his hand. 'Jerry Jacumb, Beverly Hills. And where are you from, sir?'

'I'm Canadian. Gordon Munro.' The reply was easy without being effusive.

Munro's eyes sought the bar mirror and he turned his

71

head. The two women had just appeared in the bar. Munro slid from his stool and signed the voucher.

'Nice talking with you, Mister Jacumb.'

Sheldon took his drink outside. A few people were still sitting by the pool in their swimming clothes. A soft breeze was blowing, tinged with the smell of land. Sheldon watched the trio in the bar. The girl *had* to be Munro's daughter. The way she used her hands and body indicated a close relationship. Her blonde head thrown back, she was laughing at something that he had just said. Sheldon was too far away to assess her jewellery but her clothes looked good. The overall effect was of style. There they sat, poised and sure of themselves, part of a world that Sheldon admired. A world where the wrong sort of money merely opened a trapdoor to oblivion. They were obvious elitists whose traditions and wealth appeared to be maintained without effort.

Sheldon sat at the First Officer's table for supper. The woman on his right was from Duluth, recently widowed and on the hunt for a replacement husband. Sheldon shut off his ears to her chatter and concentrated on the other tables. They were graded according to the importance of the cabins. Munro and the two women had their own seats near a window. The curtains were open, the sheets of glass reflecting the movements of the red coated waiters. Benjy was sitting across the room with Nielsen and some other people. It flashed through Sheldon's mind that though the radio operator was a hard drinker he never actually *looked* drunk.

Sheldon massaged his temples reflectively. They'd served lobster yet again and shreds of the flesh had worked themselves into the spaces between his back teeth. The neighbouring table was presided over by the purser, a mean-eyed sonofabitch who was deep in conversation with some fat-assed little priest. They hadn't stopped talking since they had sat down to eat. Sheldon picked through the cheeseboard, waiting for Benjy to finish his meal. It was after ten before Benjy rose. Sheldon signed for his half bottle of wine and followed. The mariachi band was still playing. People were on the dance floor. There was no one upstairs in the corridors. Sheldon turned the handle of one-five-six. The room was thick with the fumes of Benjy's cigar. He was sitting in one of the armchairs, his feet up on the other. Sheldon removed them.

'Was that champagne you were drinking?'

'Nielsen bought it.' Benjy banged his midriff. 'All those goddamn bubbles.'

'The money he got, he can afford to buy champagne,' Sheldon said sourly. 'Munro took the hook like a live one. I was watching his eyes all the time. You could see the fucker thinking.'

Benjy nodded. 'Pick him up again in the morning. If he goes he'll go quickly. I know the type. When the moment's right, I'll drop the poke for you.'

Sheldon's chair scraped back over the carpet. 'I'll have to wait until he's alone. He's generally with those women.'

'You'll find him,' Benjy said easily. 'The boat's not that big. The chick *is* his daughter by the way.'

Sheldon's eyes widened. 'How the hell would you know that?'

'Nielsen danced with her last night.'

'*Nielsen?*' Sheldon's expression was disbelieving.

'A courtesy thing. It would be hard for her to refuse, I guess, though she did the next time he asked.'

Sheldon yawned. 'The other one, the old woman. She's just down the corridor. We'll have to be careful.'

'Indeed,' said Benjy. 'Sweet dreams, Sheldon, and keep your hands outside the sheets.'

SIX

Sunday dawned cloudless with the M.V. *Skagerrak* a couple of hundred miles north of Puerto Rico. Russell took his breakfast in his room, drinking no more than a cup of coffee. The girls who ran room service could be finks and a priest about to say mass shouldn't be laying into ham and eggs. Messages had been coming over the p.a. system announcing that eleven o'clock mass would be celebrated by Father Mitrega, S.J. in the theatre. All Catholics were cordially invited to attend.

Russell shaved, careful about getting off the stubble he sometimes left in his chin creases. He was sixty-four, he thought with bilious disapproval, grossly overweight and making a jackass out of himself. But the rehearsals with Drury had given him a kind of confidence and he intended to give a good performance. He had taken it easy with the liquor the previous night but his mouth was unnaturally dry. He poured more coffee and sat down staring out through the porthole.

It was twenty minutes past ten when somebody knocked on the door. It was the double knock used by Drury. Russell slipped the catch back. His partner was tastefully attired in blazer and white flannel trousers and smelled of eau-de-portugal.

His quick glance took in the monstrance and crucifix. 'Everything under control?'

His jovial manner scraped Russell's nerve endings. 'Sure, everything's under control. Why wouldn't it be? But I'll tell you one thing, my friend. This is definitely the last time I make a clown of myself for anybody.'

Drury shrugged. 'Nobody asked you to be a priest. I mean, you could have been a judge. You've got the figure and that big ass that comes from spending too much time sitting down. Someone was saying at breakfast that we're going to have hymns.' He looked out through the porthole, humming.

Russell's thumb bore down on his cigarette end. 'That's Voitek's idea. The sonofabitch is making a meal of it.'

Drury perched on the side of a chair, swinging a white buckskin loafer. 'Are you going to give us a sermon?'

Russell stuck his chin out pugnaciously. 'You're taking this very coolly, you know. You won't feel so smug if something goes wrong.'

'Nothing *will* go wrong,' answered Drury. 'You're too good for that. You've even had me fooled some of the time. In any case you're going to have support. Emily-May and Judy are coming.'

Russell closed his eyes and groaned. 'That makes it perfect.'

Drury's tone was light, his smile as expansive as ever. 'There *is* something else. In fact I have a pretty weird story for you.'

'Like what?' Russell demanded suspiciously. His stomach rumbled.

'Well, I was having a drink in the Terrace Bar last night, waiting for the girls to arrive. There was nobody there, just the barman and me. A red-headed guy appears, sits down and orders a drink. A couple of minutes later a second guy arrives, sits down on the other side of me and puts a magazine down on the bar.'

A sense of the familiar crept into Russell's consciousness. 'I'm getting the picture, go on.'

'So there we are, the three of us, sitting in line, just staring at one another. The red-head finishes his drink and leaves. No sooner has he gone than the other guy asks the barman if that wasn't Chester Black?'

It was twenty-five minutes to eleven. Russell started to robe himself.

'Who's Chester Black?'

Drury feigned surprise. '*The* Chester Black. The barman checks the voucher and sure enough it's him. Then his fag friend opens up his magazine and shows me this article with Chester's picture in it. Guess what it said?'

Russell turned away from the mirror. The priest's robes made him look even stouter.

'It said that a simple old brakeman on the Canadian Pacific Railroad had just won first prize in a national lottery. But he wanted to share his prize with some deserving charity.'

Drury cancelled the guess with a wave of his hand. 'No old brakeman. This was the one about the big oilman who's just hit lucky. Can you imagine it, Mark – these bums were actually hustling me!'

Russell gargled loudly and came back into the stateroom. 'So what happens now?'

Drury was quite relaxed. 'I just hang in there and wait for them to make the next move.'

Russell was filled with a sudden sense of outrage. Everything seemed to be combining in some ghastly nightmare. He cleared his throat.

'This is beautiful. In a couple of minutes I'm going to be up there mumbling in front of a bunch of people who think I'm a priest and you choose that minute to tell me you're being hustled!'

Drury put his hand on his partner's shoulder. 'You take care of one problem, I take care of the other.' He moved his hand and tweaked Russell's cheek.

Emily-May and Judy were waiting outside the entrance to the theatre wearing scarves on their heads. Someone was playing *Gounod's Ave* in a flowery fashion on the piano inside. Drury escorted the two women into the theatre. A makeshift altar had been erected in the middle of the stage, two chairs set in front of it. A waiter wearing a cassock over his black trousers sat on one, facing the congregation. The theatre was a quarter full, passengers in front, crew back under Voitek's scrutiny. Russell made his entrance at two minutes to eleven, robed and carrying the rest of his stuff in the carpet bag. There were flowers and candles on the altar. Russell arranged the monstrance and knelt in prayerful attitude. It was an obvious effort for him to genuflect. His face was very red as he made the first announcement in a voice that was slightly shaky.

'Our first hymn is one that I'm sure is dear to all our hearts. *Daily, daily, sing to Mary!* You'll find it on page one-two-four in your hymnals.'

The congregation rose and Drury sneaked a look right and left. Judy was miles away while Emily-May's face was unreadable. The hymn ended, Russell gathered pace. Drury did his best to keep up in the missal but his friend was flying. A second hymn was sung and followed by a general shuffling of feet. Minutes later the mass was over. Russell placed a biretta on his bald head and turned to face the congregation.

'I wouldn't want you to leave without saying how much I've enjoyed celebrating holy mass with you. May God bless you all!'

'It's gone to his head,' Emily-May said in a whisper. She appeared to be right for Russell had stationed himself at the exit and was shaking hands with people who were leaving.

'Thank you, Father,' Emily-May said sweetly when they reached the door.

Drury walked the two women out onto the sunlit deck. 'I'll be back in a minute,' he said and retraced his steps. Russell had already gone. The purser was standing in the theatre entrance with the carpet bag at his feet. He stood aside to let Drury pass.

'I was looking for Father Mitrega,' Drury explained. 'I didn't get a proper chance to thank him.'

'You enjoyed the service?'

'Very much,' answered Drury.

'You didn't notice anything strange?'

Drury's toes curled. 'I don't understand.'

Voitek's manner was confidential. 'That mass wasn't the one that he usually says. I think he's a rebel. The Tridentine Mass,' he said significantly.

Drury went back to the women. 'I'm going to have to leave you two for a bit. I'll get you at lunch, OK?'

He called Russell from his room. 'A great performance. You deserve an Oscar.'

He sat for a while thinking, more concerned at the idea of being hustled than he had shown. There was no room for two teams to operate on the same boat. The dangers implicit were obvious. The thing for him to do now was to play it by ear and seek to turn the situation to his advantage. There could be no more slipping in and out of Mark's room. Communications between them had to be made by telephone.

He brushed his hair for the second time that morning, bought a Berkley mystery at the news-stand and took it up to the Bridge Deck. There were seats and parasols there and the pool was directly below. Beyond the pool, a couple of men in swimming trunks were potting clay pigeons fired from a trap. Drury settled himself comfortably under the striped parasol. It was half an hour later when Jacumb appeared, wearing Bermuda shorts and a Lacoste top. He drifted along the deck, making a show of interest in the pigeon shooters before seeing Drury. He ambled across, smiling.

'Hi there! Do you mind if I join you?'

'Help yourself.' Drury put down his book.

'I looked for you earlier,' said Jacumb, stretching his legs.

'Yes?' said Drury. He wondered how the pitch would be made.

Jacumb was sighting down at his ankle. 'Do you happen to be a bridge player? I'm trying to make up a four.'

'Poker's my game,' said Drury. There was a kind of silky decadence about the other man, something that Fellini might have portrayed in a film.

He showed small white teeth. 'It's a funny thing. I

booked this cruise after a hernia operation. It never occurred to me that I might get bored. Right now I'm beginning to wonder. Is that your daughter with you?'

Drury decided to shorten the opening process. 'That's my daughter. I know what you mean about boredom. This is my fifth cruise in as many years. I started just the moment I sold out. When you've been running a family business with a payroll of two thousand men it comes as a shock to find yourself suddenly doing nothing.'

The Winchester cracked on the deck below. Jacumb's gaze followed the fall of the shards. His voice was as delicate as a mosquito's probe. 'What kind of business were you in?'

Drury ran through the question, feeling perverse. 'No, I find that a cruise sets me up for the year. I enjoy the sun and you sometimes get to meet interesting people.'

Jacumb was clearly too smart to push his previous enquiry. Both men were silent for a while. When Drury next glanced up from his book, the red-head had appeared from nowhere and was esconced under a parasol at the next table. Things began to happen quickly. Jacumb left to go to the john. The red-head was smoking a cigarette, scribbling as he consulted some papers on the table in front of him. He collected the papers and walked away, crossing Jacumb who was returning. Jacumb bent abruptly and held a piece of paper towards Drury without even glancing at it.

'You dropped something,' he said.

Drury opened the folded paper. It was a cable that purported to have been handed into the London office on the previous evening and received aboard the *Skagerrak* at 0912 that morning. The cable was addressed to Chester Black and the text read

> Steelgrey tests positive stop Estimate yield
> thirty thousand bills Carey

Drury shook his head. 'This isn't mine.' He made no move to return the cable.

Jacumb looked unsure. 'Then whose can it be?'

'I've no idea,' said Drury and dropped the cable in his blazer pocket. It was difficult not to show his amusement. Jacumb barely had his bewilderment under control. Drury knew how he must be feeling. There was nothing in the rule book that dealt with Drury's behaviour. He was supposed to have returned the cable either to Jacumb or to its rightful owner. Drury rose.

'I'll see you later no doubt,' he said pleasantly and walked off without looking back. Up in his stateroom he took another look at the cable. Either it *had* been sent from London or they had got to the radio operator aboard ship. He made certain that the door was locked, yanked free a corner of the carpet and hid the cable underneath. Then he pulled back a chair to cover the carpet. He called the girl in the Bureau.

'This is Gordon Munro in one-zero-one. I'd like the number of Mister Jerry Jacumb's stateroom, please.'

He dialled the number, speaking very quietly when the phone was lifted at the other end.

'I want you to listen carefully. Get hold of Mister Chester Black, take him to your cabin and wait there until I arrive. Is that clear?'

There was complete silence at the Jacumb end of the line. Then his voice sounded in a mixture of surprise and belligerence.

'Just what the hell are you talking about? Who is this anyway?'

'Gordon Munro,' Drury said smoothly. 'And I'm talking about a confidence trick. Now get off the line and do as I say.'

He gave them half an hour then went down to the Bridge Deck. The door to Jacumb's cabin was unlocked, both men were inside, the red-head sitting in an armchair, Jacumb leaning against the wall. Drury lowered himself into the other chair. Neither man spoke. The first round was clearly his.

'Right,' said Drury. 'I'm glad to see that you boys are behaving sensibly. Let me give you some idea of how things stand. In the first place you were unlucky to pick on me. It means you could be in very bad trouble.'

Jacumb's face was sullen. The red-head answered. 'Just who the fuck are you, anyway?'

Drury distributed his weight comfortably. 'I recognized you two boys as hustlers the moment that I set eyes on you. And that's bad. You'll have to revamp your act.'

The red-head flushed under the freckles. 'What are you, kidding? What kind of bluff do you think you're pulling?'

'Bluff?' Drury put his head on one side and looked at them both. 'You're here, aren't you?'

The red-head shrugged. 'I don't know what your game is but you're bullshitting, friend. Now I'll tell you what you do, you back off and behave yourself. It's you who could get yourself into a whole lot of trouble, know what I mean?'

'No,' said Drury. 'Tell me!'

'You're out of your depth,' said Jacumb, coming off the wall.

'No, no,' Drury said mildly. They were getting surer of themselves. 'You guys don't seem to understand. Look, I'm prepared to gamble that your passports wouldn't stand a close investigation and there's this matter of the cable. If I do start talking, the bulls are going to drag you off the boat in irons. And for all I know, you could be wanted. You've certainly got rapsheets.'

'What is this?' asked the red-head. 'Some kind of a shakedown?'

'We're getting close,' Drury said approvingly. 'I'm assuming that you've got the radio room straight. Remember, at all times I want the truth.'

The two men exchanged glances. The red-head nodded.

'Fair enough,' said Drury. 'Now that we've established contact, so to speak, I'll leave you to think things over. Either you play ball or I carry the whole mess to the captain and let him sort things out. It's entirely up to you.

81

I'll be back here at seven for your answer. And have the radio operator here.' He smiled and went out.

SEVEN

The door closed behind Drury leaving the sound of laughter drifting up through the open portholes. Benjy shook his head disbelievingly.

'*Shit!*'

Sheldon's face tightened with rage and frustration. 'You and your goddamn vibes! This fucker's going to have us busted, do you realize that?'

But Benjy was thinking. 'Settle down,' he said, holding up a hand. 'Maybe he's one of these law and order freaks. You know the kind, stand too long under a lamp post and he calls the cops.'

He was casting in all directions and both of them knew it. 'That's crap,' said Sheldon. 'This guy's no freak. How do we know that he isn't a cop?'

'A *crooked* cop?' Benjy looked interested. 'Then what is his angle?'

Sheldon developed a light stutter. 'S-s-crewing us is his angle.'

Benjy took a turn to the bathroom and back. A picture had formed in his mind. A cigar spiralling through the darkness, the sound of a body hitting the water lost in the throbbing of the ship's engines.

'Maybe we should anchor the bastard to the bottom of the ocean.'

'Aiee!' said Sheldon closing his eyes. 'This is what he calls good thinking! What do we do, Benjy, tip him over the side when he isn't looking. What are you, suddenly, Murder Incorporated?'

'Shut up,' said Benjy, clicking his fingers. 'If it wasn't for that cable he wouldn't have a thing. Why didn't you get it back from him?'

Sheldon's small face was savage. He came a couple of steps closer to his brother.

'Because he put it in his pocket is why! What was I supposed to do, knock him down and drag it away from him? In any case it isn't just the cable. He's right about the passports. Those books will never stand a check in Washington which means that the Feds will have jurisdiction. They'll have us out on McNeil, Benjy, with a bunch of geeks and dope fiends.'

Benjy was still pacing, snapping his fingers. 'Someone's going to have to talk to Nielsen.'

Sheldon sat down heavily. 'We'll be in Haiti tomorrow. Maybe we should make a run for it, Benjy. Start hopping the islands.'

'Sheldon, Sheldon!' Benjy wagged his head sadly. 'Your co-operation is turning out to be nil. What do you think we are, hopping islands, kangaroos? This guy's coming back here at seven and make no mistake, if he *does* go to the Captain we'll leave the boat in chains.'

His brother seemed bereft of ideas. 'All this stuff about the radio room. What does he want with the radio room?'

'We'll find out soon enough.' Benjy sat down in turn. 'I'm wondering whether he could be one of the mob. Some old-timer we never heard of.'

Sheldon rejected the idea. 'He's something to do with the law. A district attorney, maybe. That's it, Benjy! A district attorney on a cruise with his daughter.'

'They don't have district attorneys in Canada,' Benjy answered.

'So what? Whatever they call them there. He's tried a few con cases, heard the way they go. That's why he was able to pick up on the pitch.'

Benjy's voice was cool. 'So why doesn't he go to the Captain?'

Sheldon's shoulders rose and fell. 'What do we do, Benjy?'

Benjy was beginning to recover his poise. 'We use our heads, Shel. Stay with this guy and whatever he wants we outsmart him. We can run rings round an old fart like that.'

'I dunno,' said Sheldon. 'What happens with Nielsen?'

Benjy thought about it, but not for too long. 'I'm going to tell him if we fall, he falls. Don't worry about Nielsen, he's the least of our problems. I'll deal with it now.'

It was after four o'clock and the Main Hall was crowded. The door of the radio room was locked but the shutter was up. Benjy poked his head over the counter.

'Open up!' he ordered.

Nielsen reached across and turned the key. Benjy slipped in and stood so that he was out of sight from people in the Hall. He could smell the liquor on Nielsen's breath.

'We're in bad trouble,' Benjy said quietly. 'Somebody's got hold of the cable.'

Nielsen's eyes slid sideways. 'What cable's that?'

Benjy's voice hardened. 'Now listen, asshole! There's only one radio room on this ship, only one lush playing around with cables. You'd better get this straight in your mind. The guy wants to see us at seven o'clock. If we're not there he's going to take a walk to the bridge. And if we fall, buster, we take you with us.'

Nielsen's face reddened. 'I should have known better. "A couple of hotshots from the Coast" he said! Thanks a lot, Lansky!'

'You think Lansky did *us* a favour?' Benjy's contempt was plain. 'You no good bum, you! And just in case you're thinking about copping out I'm personally prepared to swear that I paid you money to take cables. Seven o'clock, room one-five-nine.'

Sheldon was sitting wrapped in his white towelling robe, like a beaten fighter at the end of a bout.

'We're going to have to keep a close eye on that bastard,'

85

Benjy remarked. 'He's cranking up courage to do something.'

'I say run and the hell with it,' said Sheldon looking up.

Benjy slipped into his big brother pose. 'Listen, Shel, you and I are pros, right?'

Sheldon shook off Benjy's hand. 'So?'

'So we can handle a bum like Nielsen. He's shit-scared anyway.'

'So am I,' Sheldon said morosely.

'Garbage!' said Benjy. 'You've always got nerve in the pinch. Munro doesn't look like blowing the whistle on us, right? Which makes him one of us. Think about it, Sheldon.'

'I've thought,' said Sheldon. 'But it doesn't make me feel any better.'

Benjy smiled at his brother. When you got a head of steam on Sheldon, you had to keep it running.

'We *know* thieves,' said Benjy. 'We know the way their minds work. This guy may not know it but he's standing way too close to the flames.'

The library was at the end of a corridor that was unused during the day. Other than the library, there was nothing there except storerooms and the casino which only opened at ten o'clock at night. Drury turned the handle and stepped into the musty odour of seldom read books. There were Tauchnitz editions of the classics on the shelves, a complete set of the *Encyclopaedia Britannica*, stacks of travel and guide-books, paperbacks and novels left by a generation of passengers. Six portholes shed light on the reading tables. It was quiet in the room, the only noise the distant hum of the engines.

Drury sat down at one of the tables and took a cigar from his case. He had a feeling of certainty, a gut feeling as the current jargon had it. It was a throw-back to the old days when he'd put a foal or yearling into the sales and had known that it would make good money. What he was experiencing now was the same kind of feeling. He had already made up his mind what to do. What he hadn't yet decided was how precisely to do it. He spent the next hour studying up-to-date guide-books dealing with Haiti and Puerto Rico. It was after six when he finally went upstairs to his cabin. He tapped on Jacumb's door at seven o'clock exactly. This time there was someone else present. A tall man with ragged grey hair and broken veined face was sitting on one of the chairs. He wore a Marconi flash on the sleeve of his tunic and was chewing gum with nervous intensity. Jacumb was in a towelling robe.

Drury nodded all round. 'Are we ready to get things moving?'

No one answered so Drury pointed at the red-head. 'You want to tell me your real name?'

'Take a hike,' the red-head said sullenly.

'Fair enough!' Drury's manner was amiable. 'So it's Mister Black and Mister Jacumb. How about you, friend?'

The radio man's voice was husky. 'Nielsen.'

There was no room for Drury except on the bed. 'It isn't just that I'm older than you guys, I'm smarter, too. That's something it'll pay you to keep in your heads at all times.'

The red-head constituted himself spokesman. 'You haven't brought us here to tell us how smart you are. What's the scenario?'

Drury tried to sound like a man who was a little too sure of himself. It was important at this juncture to fuel these kids' basic contempt for him.

'You guys are going to help me rob a bank. It's something I always wanted to do. You've provided me with the key.'

Benjy Field's face reddened in the sudden hush. 'Are you putting us on or something? *Rob a bank*? What do we do for a getaway, take to sea in a lifeboat?'

'Don't be argumentative,' Drury said sharply. 'I could be playing this the hard way. Fear's about the strongest incentive there is. You'll roll over when I say so. But I like to think myself a fair man so I'm throwing you guys a lifeline. What's your first name?' He was looking at the radio operator.

'Ed.' Nielsen licked his lips as though he had just pleaded guilty to something.

'How come you know this pair of rogues?' asked Drury, nodding at the other two.

Nielsen stayed silent. It was Benjy who answered, his face frankly hostile. 'What are you, some kind of dingbat trying to pull stuff like this? Look I can have you wasted the moment we put foot on dry land.'

'That's a useful thing to know,' said Drury. 'I'll keep it at the front of my mind. What time do you go on duty, Ed?'

Nielsen wet his lips cautiously. 'Eight o'clock in the morning.'

'Who works with you?'

'There's only me this trip. The trainee's out with appendicitis.'

'OK,' said Drury. 'Now listen very carefully, Ed. I'll be coming down to your office first thing in the morning with a cable. The reply will come to the Hastrupbank downstairs. I want a copy of that reply just as soon as it arrives. Understood?'

Nielsen licked his lips. 'You want *me* to do this? Give you a copy of a cable to the bank?'

'That's right,' said Drury. 'It's more or less the same sort of thing that you've been doing, isn't it?'

Nielsen swallowed hard. He was having difficulty in finding a place to rest his gaze.

'That's all you want from me?'

'Wrong,' said Drury. 'That's just the beginning, Ed. You and I are going to work together closely. Are you in charge of the records?'

'I already told you. There is only me.'

The Field brothers were watching attentively. 'Then there should be no problems, Ed,' Drury went on. 'I hope so for your sake. Because if anything *should* go wrong, it's going to be your ass. Now is all that quite clear?'

Nielsen moved his head as if it had just acquired additional weight.

'Sure, the cable. The copy of the cable.'

'Then we needn't detain you any longer,' Drury said, smiling. 'There'll be other things for you to do, Ed. Other things for everyone to do.'

Words formed in Nielsen's head but they never emerged. He left the room without replying. Drury leaned forward, placing his hands on his knees.

'OK, now we can get down to cases. I told you back there that I thought myself a fair man. Don't believe a word of it. I'm a mean-hearted sonofabitch and I don't like your style. In fact I don't like anything about either of you. But in spite of that I'm going to make you an offer. You'll take it because there's no alternative. Rather, there *is* an alternative – whatever you get for tampering with the cable service, attempted grand larceny . . . do you want me to go on?'

'Just get to the point,' said Benjy. 'What kind of offer?'

'A generous one,' answered Drury. 'I'm going to give you guys ten grand apiece and there'll be ten for Nielsen. It'll pay for your trip and leave change. Not only that, the experience should be worth a fortune.'

Benjy's face was suspicious. 'And what do we have to do for this?'

'What you have to do is exactly what I say. No more no less, otherwise . . . ' Drury drew his finger across his throat. 'The first job is this. There's a priest on the cruise, a little fat guy wears a panama hat. Do you know who I mean?'

Sheldon found his voice at last. 'You and your fucking vibes,' he complained, looking at his brother.

'Sits at the purser's table?' queried Benjy.

'Right.' Drury continued. 'His name's Father Mitrega. I want Mister Jacumb here to pick this priest up and steer him to Mister Black. Mister Black is playing the part of a rich Catholic known for his largesse to the Church. Can you do a rich Catholic, Mister Black?'

'Hold it,' said Benjy. 'Let me get this straight. You want us to beat a *priest* for money?'

'I want you to *give* a priest money,' Drury corrected. 'To be precise, one hundred thousand dollars. But there is a proviso.'

The Californians exchanged rapid glances. 'What proviso?' asked Benjy.

'Father Mitrega has to pick up half a million dollars from a bank.'

Benjy almost choked on the sum. 'Half a ... it just doesn't sound ... '

'It's your job to *make* it sound right,' said Drury smoothly. 'You ever hear of a priest refusing to take money? You're giving, remember, not taking.'

Sheldon broke in. 'My head's going round here, let's get something straight. You want us to con this priest into picking up half a million bucks and handing it over to us?'

'Something along those lines,' said Drury. 'The hook is that he gets a hundred grand for his trouble. What I suggest is that you put your heads together and think up some tax dodge story. Even a priest loves a tax dodge story.'

'And where does this money come from?' Benjy spoke slowly, almost languorously.

Drury stood up, brushing the cigar ash from his blazer. 'We'll get to that later. Don't worry, you'll be told whatever is necessary. I'm glad to see you boys acting so sensibly. You're brash and entirely without any style but the idea of having you thrown in the pokey affords me no pleasure at all. I'll expect one of you to call me with the number of Father Mitrega's passport before we get to Port-au-Prince.'

It took Drury half an hour to locate Russell lying flat on his back on a *chaise-longue*, his face covered with his panama hat. Drury lolled on a rail nearby and cleared his throat but the noise was lost amid the yelling of a teenage couple fooling around on the springboard. They were burned as brown as Brazilians and noisy. The pool itself was empty except for an oversized and overheated blonde floating on a sagging ring. Drury pulled another cigar from his case and moved upwind. When the breeze was blowing in the right direction, he lit the cigar. Russell moved like a fox getting scent of a hen. His feet twitched and then his hand. Then, very carefully, he lifted the brim of his hat and peered out from under it. Drury nodded in the direction of the cabins. Russell's head shot back, this time like a tortoise. After a while, he sat up straight, wiped his forehead and walked off towards the lifts. Drury dragged a couple of invigorating breaths into his lungs and followed his partner.

Russell opened the door guardedly. 'What are you doing here again? We're supposed to be strangers.'

'No one saw me come in,' Drury assured him. 'I had to see you. I've just left the three of them. The radio operator looked as though Death was whispering in his ear and the other two don't look much better. You could say, Mark, that we've caught them wrongfooted.'

Russell had already removed his clerical jacket and collar. He had acquired an icebox from somewhere and had it filled with cans of Australian lager. He pulled the tab on one and threw another to Drury.

'How'd you feel?' asked Drury.

'Shitty,' said Russell. 'That purser follows me around like a goddamn hound. Not only that, I never did like villainy that I don't understand. I almost had to sit down when you told me we were robbing a bank.'

The chilled beer made the roof of Drury's mouth cold. 'That wouldn't make much of a change. You've been sitting down or lying down for the last sixty odd years. That's one of the reasons you're fat. That and greediness. What exactly is it that's worrying you, Mark?'

'What's worrying me?' Russell's mouth widened without humour. 'All the time I know you, you're still doing the same old crap, Phil. The girl's tied to the railroad track. The down express is hitting ninety miles an hour. And what does Phil Drury say "What exactly is it that's worrying you, Miss?" Shit, I'm an old man, not some kid with a snoutful of speed.'

Drury dropped his empty beer-can in the basket, reversed the chair and straddled it. 'For a man of God you show little faith.'

Russell's fat hand trembled violently. 'For a man of God I seem to be running into plenty of trouble. Show me a mark and I can handle him, but what the hell do I know about robbing banks? When it comes to that sort of thing I've led a sheltered life.'

'You will not listen,' Drury reproved. 'This is no vulgar rip-off that I am concocting. Hold it under the glass and you'll see its beauty.'

'Outrageous bullshit!' said Russell. 'I just do not understand you. I've taken a close look at this trio. One of the kids is a weasel-toothed degenerate and the radio operator's a lush. Please tell me what we're doing with people like this.'

'We're teaching the buggers a lesson,' said Drury. 'And at the same time we're helping ourselves to half a million dollars. Those kids are a blessing in disguise, Mark.'

Russell's face looked as though he'd bitten hard on an abscess. '"Helping ourselves", he says. We're into some outrageous bullshit about robbing a bank and he calls it "helping ourselves".'

Drury's cigar was getting oily. He laid the butt to rest. 'You've got the mind of a loan-shark, Russell. Will you listen to what I have to say or not?'

Russell finished his beer and wiped his mouth on the back of his hand. A wisp of hair standing straight up at the back of his head gave him the look of a bereft banshee.

'I guess there has to be a first time for everything,' he said grudgingly.

Drury explained his scheme in detail. 'It wouldn't work on shore,' he concluded. 'At least not in this way. Urgent transfers are made by phone and confirmed by telex. Even that isn't foolproof. You can tap the lines.'

Russell's manner had taken on definite interest. 'Are you saying that there's no check on a ship-to-shore operation?'

'No, I'm not,' answered Drury. 'They check too. Know something about these telex lines, Mark? There was this long piece in the papers a month or so ago. Some system consultant was pointing out flaws. It seems that all you need is a four hundred dollar kit to tap the telex line and you're in business.'

Russell's manner approached reverence. 'You mean that you can actually *buy* stuff like that?'

'Apparently. Any electronics store in New York stocks it. What you have to do is crack the bankers' code and feed in your own requirements.'

Russell clutched his head with fat fingers. 'We were born fifty years too soon.'

'We've got the edge in experience,' said Drury. 'The thing is that a bank aboard ship uses a different system. They have to rely on the phone or on cables.'

'But they still check,' Russell objected. 'Surely one bank'll check with another somehow?'

'That's exactly right,' said Drury, producing the final rabbit from the hat. 'And the man in the bank downstairs gets the cables we want him to get. *Compris*?'

For the first time Russell looked reasonably happy. He kicked off his shoes and flexed his toes.

'How long will it take the bank to realize they've been had?'

Drury's eyes sought the ceiling. 'Let's be conservative about this. Once we're past the teller in San Juan it'll be at least two weeks before the shit hits the fan. We'll be off the island the same day.'

'Half a million?' Russell's tone was doubtful.

'Chicken feed,' Drury retorted. 'They're shooting these amounts around fifty times a day.'

incentive there is. You'll roll over when I say so. But I like to think myself a fair man so I'm throwing you guys a lifeline. What's your first name?' He was looking at the radio operator.

'Ed.' Nielsen licked his lips as though he had just pleaded guilty to something.

'How come you know this pair of rogues?' asked Drury, nodding at the other two.

Nielsen stayed silent. It was Benjy who answered, his face frankly hostile. 'What are you, some kind of dingbat trying to pull stuff like this? Look I can have you wasted the moment we put foot on dry land.'

'That's a useful thing to know,' said Drury. 'I'll keep it at the front of my mind. What time do you go on duty, Ed?'

Nielsen wet his lips cautiously. 'Eight o'clock in the morning.'

'Who works with you?'

'There's only me this trip. The trainee's out with appendicitis.'

'OK,' said Drury. 'Now listen very carefully, Ed. I'll be coming down to your office first thing in the morning with a cable. The reply will come to the Hastrupbank downstairs. I want a copy of that reply just as soon as it arrives. Understood?'

Nielsen licked his lips. 'You want *me* to do this? Give you a copy of a cable to the bank?'

'That's right,' said Drury. 'It's more or less the same sort of thing that you've been doing, isn't it?'

Nielsen swallowed hard. He was having difficulty in finding a place to rest his gaze.

'That's all you want from me?'

'Wrong,' said Drury. 'That's just the beginning, Ed. You and I are going to work together closely. Are you in charge of the records?'

'I already told you. There is only me.'

The Field brothers were watching attentively. 'Then there should be no problems, Ed,' Drury went on. 'I hope

'I wish . . . ' he began then shook his head. 'The hell with it.'

'You'd have had to tell the kid sooner or later.' Russell's tone was sympathetic.

But it wasn't so. At least he had never planned it that way. At the back of his mind had been a straight con pulled off under Judy's very nose without her being aware of it, the mark moved on five thousand miles and no need for explanations. They could have left the cruise with no one the wiser. His dilemma had always been the same. He could never find the courage to risk the loss of her love. Now he had no choice. The decision had been made for him. He changed the subject deliberately.

'These punks'll come at you tomorrow. I've given them a deadline. Don't make it too easy for them. Find a couple of moral scruples.'

Russell tilted his head back and drank from the beer-can. 'You keep calling them kids. These are grown men, Phil, and dangerous. With half a million bucks at stake they're going to be flashing all over the place.'

'I know it,' said Drury and talked again without interruption for a further ten minutes.

Russell's face spread in a fat grin. 'Say no more! This is dangerous bullshit, but I'll go along with it.'

'Good,' said Drury and looked at his watch.

Russell eyed his partner curiously. 'You ever think about the old days, Phil?'

'Not if I can help it!' Drury's tone was light but he meant exactly what he said. Few of the memories were pleasant.

'Acapulco?'

Acapulco was different. Helen. The beach. The monstrous surf thundering in. A new life about to begin. It was all a long time ago, but sure he remembered.

'They tell me it's changed,' he said. 'But then what the hell hasn't? You – me – everything's changed.'

'You sound like Walter Cronkite on a bad night,' said

Russell and opened the door. He peered along the passage and jerked his head. 'It's clear. I'll talk to you later.'

It was five minutes past eight the following morning. The deck had been hosed down and was steaming gently in the early sunshine. Heels thudded on the diving board followed by the sound of a body breaking the surface of the water. Drury reached the bottom of the staircase. The radio room was the last door in the row of shops and offices. It stood ajar though the service counter was closed. Hoovers were droning along the corridors. The only people in sight were deckhands polishing brass and the girls from room service carrying breakfast trays. Drury pushed the door open.

Nielsen was in his shirt-sleeves, his tunic draped on the chair behind him. The smell of whisky was still on him and his eyes looked as though he had slept badly. Drury closed the door. 'Everything under control?'

Nielsen's jaw muscles tightened. 'Look, can't we skip the chatter and get this over?'

Drury pushed out a hand. 'Cable form.'

Nielsen passed the pad over the desk. 'I'm screwed if I go for this and I'm screwed if I don't. It's a great future.'

'That's what happens when you cut your own throat,' said Drury. He completed the cable and read it through.

Amibank Bahnhofstrasse Zürich

Transfer ten thousand dollars U.S. soonest my favour Kastrupbank aboard Danish-Lloyd M.V. *Skagerrak* stop

Acknowledge receipt instructions by phone BJO 1956

Nielsen read the cable and frowned. 'I can't send this, not the way it is!'

'Why not?' Drury demanded.

Nielsen took a drag on his cigarette. 'Regulations is why not. The name of the sender has to figure on the form.'

'That's bullshit,' said Drury. 'You *are* the regulations! Just send the cable, son.'

He sat watching as Nielsen adjusted the headphones. A

high-pitched whine filled the room and then dwindled. The radio operator spoke into the mouthpiece, giving his call sign. He repeated the message, spelling names twice and reiterating the amounts. A red light went out and he wiped his neck.

'God*damn*!' he said with quiet desperation.

'You'll make out,' Drury said leisurely. Nielsen would do as he was told although every step took him in deeper. 'It's not far off one o'clock Swiss time,' said Drury. 'My bank'll probably answer before they close. Someone will call and ask for the number on the cable. BJO 1956. I'll be up in my cabin.'

Nielsen shook his head. 'This isn't going to work, you know.'

'You'd better hope that it does,' said Drury and heaved himself out of the chair. 'From now on I want a copy of everything that comes into this place or goes out of it. As soon as you get them, remember!'

Judy was already down at breakfast, cool-looking in sea green cotton. The first flush of sunburn had already faded on her face. She had eaten her grapefruit, nothing else.

'What happened?' she asked, looking up as he took his seat. 'Didn't you sleep well?'

'Not too well.' He poured himself coffee.

Judy put her head on one side. 'Is something bothering you?'

He smiled. 'Being asked questions like that is what's bothering me.'

'And grouchy with it!' His daughter had her mother's brusque manner in this sort of situation. 'It looks as though I made the wrong decision after all,' she said. 'I should never have come, obviously. You'd have been happier on your own.'

He put his coffee cup down and took her hand. 'That's nonsense.' Thought of the coming showdown saddened him. What he had to tell would jolt her hard.

She left her hand where it was for a while and then gently removed it.

'Poor Papa! I really bug you at times, don't I? I'll let you finish your breakfast in peace.'

He watched her as far as the door but she didn't look back. He wiped his mouth on his napkin, no longer hungry. He still retained the ability to forget irrelevancies and bring his mind to bear on a single problem. The only worry he took to the bank was the immediate one. Drury used the door instead of going to the counter. A girl in a flowered dress and a hair band turned in surprise.

'I'm Gordon Munro in room one-zero-one. I'd like to speak with the manager,' Drury said courteously.

His manner had obviously dispelled her initial reluctance. She knocked on an inner door and then turned towards Drury. 'Will you come through, Mister Munro?'

It was a large room with a miniature strongroom built into one wall. Behind steel bars were two oversize safes. They were protected by all the usual devices but now they stood open. A middle-aged man in his shirt-sleeves rose and put out his hand. He was sandy haired and wearing gold-rimmed spectacles.

'Good morning, Mister Munro. I'm Axel Tefler. How can I help you?' His fluent English was only slightly accented.

Drury took the chair that was offered. Currency of several kinds and denominations was stacked in trays on a table near the door. Drury made himself comfortable. He had dealt with a thousand Teflers in his life. The trick was to make them feel important.

'I find I'm going to need more funds than I anticipated on the cruise. I've cabled my bank in Zürich to send me ten thousand dollars.'

Tefler cracked a knuckle, his eyes assessing Drury. 'Yes?'

'I've asked them to make the transfer to you, to the bank.'

'No problem there, Mister Munro.' Tefler smiled faintly. 'We can let you have the cash.'

'Good,' Drury said heartily. 'I hear fine things about Kastrupbank. It's possible that I may need to have a much larger sum transferred, half a million dollars, in fact.'

The movement of the boat was making the door swing. Tefler put it on a hook.

'Yes, yes, I see. That might cause difficulties if you wanted the entire sum in cash. You see, we only carry a limited amount.'

Drury took the manager into his confidence. 'It's a business deal that may or may not jell during the trip. I'm waiting for confirmation which might come at any time. Or not at all. The one thing certain is that I wouldn't need cash.' He spread his hands and smiled.

Tefler brought his professional expertise into play. 'It sounds to me as though your best bet would be to transfer directly to San Juan or Caracas. We have branches in both cities.'

Drury shook his head. 'That would only complicate matters. I'd want the credit here on board ship where I can get at it quickly. Of course, if the amount is too large ...'

Drury could hear the whirr of the calculator in the outer office. The girl had removed the trays of currency. Tefler ran hard to support his bank's reputation.

'Indeed no, Mister Munro. As long as we're not talking in terms of actual cash. We could always give you a banker's draft or transfer the money again. Paperwork, that's all it is.'

Drury grinned amiably. 'It may not be necessary. Everything depends on the call I'm expecting. But the ten thousand dollars is sure. It should be through ... but you'd be a better judge of that.'

'This afternoon,' ventured Tefler. 'More likely tomorrow morning.'

Drury lowered his voice. 'It's a numbered account. BJO 1956 at the Amibank in Zürich.'

Tefler scribbled a note. 'I have your room number,

Mister Munro. I'll let you know the moment I have some news for you.' He came as far as the door with Drury, bobbed his head and went back to work.

It was busy out in the Main Hall with people cashing travellers cheques to spend in Port-au-Prince. Seeing Emily-May in the news-stand, Drury altered his course.

'I want to talk to you,' he said. 'Come into the library.' He closed the door behind them. She sat down at the reading table, her face curious. Years spent in the sun had weathered her skin and a few days' exposure to it had made her arms the colour of new acorns. There were fine pale frown lines at the edges of her eyes.

'Just what *is* going on?' she demanded. 'What have you done with Mark? I haven't set eyes on him since that performance in the church.'

'He's being careful,' said Drury. 'We've suddenly got a problem on our hands. I've been picked up by a couple of Californian con men.' He told her what had happened.

She stared disbelievingly until she realized that he was serious. Then she started to laugh, dabbing at her eyes with a handkerchief.

'Oh, Phil,' she said. 'If you could only see the look on your face! Positively outraged!'

'I was at first,' he admitted. 'But not any more. These kids are about to make our fortune.'

She listened, playing with the strap of her watch, as he explained for a second time.

'But isn't that highly dangerous?' she asked when he had finished.

'Are you talking about dangerous for Mark?'

Her voice was very quiet. 'I'm talking about dangerous for both of you, for everyone.'

'It's dangerous,' Drury admitted. 'But no more so than the original plan. We never were on a picnic. Look at it this way, the risk will be concentrated and there are plenty of built-in safety valves.'

Emily-May's violet eyes were troubled. 'The little soldier's really going to have to stick his neck out.'

'The little soldier's going to be sticking out his neck for his share of half a million,' said Drury. 'Look, honey, both of us are long out of the business and we've never taken a fall. The bulls are going to be left with no more than names and descriptions. The names are phoney and the descriptions could be of a couple of million people. The only guy really at risk is the guy in the radio room. Think about it.'

'I've thought,' she said quickly, unsmiling. 'The whole idea sends shivers down my spine, but I know what I'm going to do. Why do you need these other rogues? It seems to me that this weakens your hand considerably. Surely they'll know what's going on?'

'They'll know *part* of what's going on,' he corrected. 'We've got their key-man, that's why we need them. That and because it's better to have a sidewinder out where you can see it than under the bed. This is a new breed, Emily-May, with contempt for anyone over thirty. They don't like me or what they think I stand for and their emotions are clouding their judgement. I resent these little buggers and I'm going to beat their ass like a gong.'

She prodded at the smouldering stub in the ashtray until the last shred of tobacco was extinguished.

'Well,' she said, 'I just hope that you're right. Which brings us to the subject of Judy. What do you intend to do there?'

'I'm not sure,' he admitted.

She stared him full in the eye. 'Then you'd better be sure! You're going to have some explaining to do if we're taking off from San Juan.'

Her manner told him that whatever else *she* wasn't backing out and he was glad of it.

'I'll level with you, Emily-May,' he said. 'I don't think I've ever been so scared of anything in my life.'

'Yep,' she said briskly. 'I'm glad I never had kids. Have you any idea at all what you're going to say to her?'

It was difficult to frame the sentences even in his mind. The past was just about possible to explain but not the present. How did he tell her that at sixty-five years of age he was still a thief and a liar?

He made a gesture of defeat. 'I don't know. I just do not know.'

She inspected her face in her hand mirror then closed her bag. 'I'll tell you one thing for what it's worth, something that I learned the hard way years ago. Half-truths are a waste of time. Not only that, they have a way of springing up at you like a garden rake when you step on it. It has to be all or nothing.'

He knew exactly what she meant, but it made nothing easier. 'I'll think of something,' he said without confidence.

He found a shady spot on the Bridge Deck. They were five hours from Port-au-Prince and there was a general air of expectancy abroad. People were trying out their French on one another. Most of them seemed to have worked out some sort of itinerary and the news-stand had been doing a land office business in phrase books and maps. Drury's vantage point gave him a clear view of the deck below. Russell was down there sitting with Jacumb on one side, the red-head on the other. The three were locked in conversation. There was a touch of frenzy about Jacumb's performance. He was using his hands a lot. It looked as if Mark was giving him a hard time. Suddenly the red-head left. No sooner had he gone than Jacumb had Russell on his feet and was steering him along the deck, hanging onto his arm.

Drury smiled and picked up his book. That wouldn't last too long. Mark had no liking for walking. He read for half an hour until he heard his name being paged over the public address system.

'A telephone call for Mister Gordon Munro. Will Mister Gordon Munro please pick up the nearest courtesy phone!'

There was a phone just inside the entrance to the elevator hall. It was Jacumb.

'Do you have pencil and paper?'

'Sure,' lied Drury.

'The passport. The full name is Jerzy Mitrega and the number is two-six-three-seven-five-eight-nine.'

'Got it,' said Drury. Russell must have finally rolled over for them.

Jacumb sounded pleased with himself. 'He's hooked. He wants a new wing for the chapel at Marymount Seminary. The hundred grand will start the fund. Mister Black gets his name on a piece of marble. I'm buying the good father dinner in Port-au-Prince.'

'Good,' said Drury. 'Tell me how you get on. I'll be back in my cabin by eleven o'clock.'

One o'clock came and went and there was still no reply to his cable to the bank. It was after six o'clock in the evening in Zürich. The banks closed at four. He closed his book and went down to the restaurant. Judy was sitting alone at their table, her newspaper open at the crossword. She glanced up, smiling.

'Hi! We seem to be at cross purposes today. I already ate. I wasn't sure if you were coming down.'

He scanned the menu and settled for cold ham and an endive salad. Judy's copy of the London *Times* was a week old. He had a strong feeling that she had a good reason for being there. Like her mother, she made points with a rapier rather than a cutlass. The wine waiter was still hovering, doing his best to take a look down Judy's cleavage. Drury ordered a bottle of Perrier water.

'What is it?' Judy asked suddenly.

He broke a roll and put a piece of bread in his mouth. 'What is what?'

She put her pen away. 'Come off it, Papa. You've been like a broody hen for the last day or so.'

He nodded slowly. 'There's something I have to tell you and I don't know how to start.'

She placed both elbows on the table and framed her face in her hands. 'Shoot!'

103

His complaint about a restless night had been true. He had slept like a fox, alert to both known and unknown dangers.

'It's not the moment. It could turn into an epic. I thought we'd have a quiet meal together in Port-au-Prince.'

She turned down the corners of her mouths. 'I half-promised Emily-May.'

'So you half-keep your promise. You can meet her either before or after supper. Both, if you like. It's just that I have to be alone with you for a while.'

'It isn't going to be about a woman, is it?'

'No.'

'Money?' This was the moment when he could have shown his hand, but he lacked the guts to do so. 'It's about us really. I want you to know that you're the most important person in the whole wide world to me.'

Her face softened. 'I love you, Papa. I may not show it any too well, but I do love you.'

Their eyes held until each was satisfied. He nodded. 'Yeah! Now go find Emily-May, honey. The first launch leaves at five-thirty. I'll try to get us on it and meet you both in the Main Hall.'

She collected her bag and newspaper, blew him a kiss and sauntered away, swing-hipped and looking straight in front of her. He watched her proudly. Whatever she had done in her life she had done with enthusiasm. For her there was no such thing as a good or bad loser. She never admitted that she had lost, not even in her marriage. He pushed away his half-finished meal. Emily-May had gone to the heart of the matter. There was no room for anything except the whole truth. Anything less would only damage him even more. There were times when he had thought of finding someone like Emily-May but his thoughts always came back to Judy. The fact was that his relationship with her was more important than anything else.

The Texan girl in the Bureau was distributing tickets for the launch. She gave him three seats for the five-thirty trip.

The last launch back left at eleven-thirty and the *Skager-rak* sailed half an hour later. He went back to the Bridge Deck. No sooner had he taken off his jacket and shoes than the telephone rang. It was Nielsen.

'I've got your bank in Zürich on the line.'

There was a series of clicks and Herr Rössli came on. 'Hello, yes? Have you something to say to me, please?'

Drury gave the coded signal that identified him. The Amibank manager was a humourless man with the sparkle of processed cheese. His voice sounded worried as usual.

'I am specially calling from my home, yes? The international lines have been busy. I am very sorry.'

'Have you sent the money?' The little that Drury had eaten had left his stomach unsettled.

Rössli was determined to spell it out. 'We have received your instructions at three o'clock this afternoon by our time. I have immediately ordered the transfer via Kastrup-bank's agents here in Zürich. Do you now have advice?'

'Not yet,' said Drury. There was no public use of names. As far as the Swiss were concerned, a demand for a numbered account indicated a desire for privacy and this they respected.

'Then it is coming very soon,' said Rössli. 'Perhaps in the morning early.'

'OK,' said Drury.

'Good!' Rössli hesitated. 'So how is weather?'

'Hot,' said Drury. 'Goodbye and thanks.' He put the phone back on the rest and retrieved the cable he had hidden under the carpet. He placed it in an envelope addressed to himself care of Judy and stretched out on the bed again.

He had never made the mistake of underestimating the opposition and had no intention of doing so now. Looking back on things, it had never been easy to score. No matter how greedy the mark, someone always seemed to be around counselling caution, usually a wife or girlfriend. Worst was the protective bank manager. This was when the steerer would have to move in with the mark, hold his hand and stoke his greed, a fellow conspirator. The old classic con tricks had been polished by generations of grafters and were based in the larceny hidden in a sucker's heart. A really honest man could never be beaten.

He flexed his thigh tentatively. He hadn't been on a horse in four months and his riding muscles were getting flabby. The phone rang again. Nielsen's voice sounded as though he had the mouthpiece cupped with his hand.

'Your money's in.' Five minutes later Tefler was on the line.

'Mister Munro? Your transfer is through. I wonder if you'd mind coming down and signing a couple of papers. And will you bring your passport, please? We need the details for our records.'

Drury pulled on his clothes and brushed his hair, looking at himself in the mirror. Younger than his years, maybe, but for those kids he was still an old fart who should be out at grass. He put the Munro passport in his pocket and posted the envelope in the Main Hall. Nielsen was leaning over the counter of the radio room trying to attract his attention. Drury took the sealed buff envelope and walked the few yards to the bank. The girl showed him into Tefler's office. The manager pushed a chair in Drury's direction.

'You remembered to bring your passport?'

Drury produced the blue booklet. Tefler called and the girl appeared.

'Take Mister Munro's passport, Sally. You want the name, number and date of issue for the blue twelve forms. OK?'

He nodded confidentially. 'All this is strictly for our records, Mister Drury. I'm afraid we're not like the Swiss. An account has to have a name.'

Drury scribbled a signature twice and put his pen away. 'Do I detect a note of disapproval there?'

Tefler's expression was horrified. 'Good God, no!'

'I'm glad,' said Drury, but he didn't sound too convinced. 'Is that all?'

Tefler was clearly worried. 'I hope you don't think . . .

I mean I've always been a strong supporter of confidential banking.'

'I'm sure,' said Drury, standing. 'That's all, is it?'

'Absolutely,' said Tefler. 'The girl will give you your passport back.' He opened a drawer and produced a South Korean copy of a Cartier lighter. 'With the compliments of Hastrupbank. Please let me know how I can be of further help, Mister Munro.'

'I'll let you know about the other matter just as soon as I hear,' said Drury.

'Anything the bank can do,' assured Tefler. 'We'll be glad to be of service.'

'I mustn't miss the first launch,' smiled Drury. 'Do you get ashore on these occasions?'

'Not unless I can help it,' said Tefler. 'I'm afraid there's nothing about the Caribbean that I find exciting.'

'The Bankers Club in Caracas might give you a new outlook,' said Drury. 'We'll have lunch there and thanks for your help!'

The warm flood after the icy douche restored Tefler's self-possession. 'I'll be happy to join you, Mister Munro. An experience I've dreamed about!'

Upstairs in his cabin, Drury opened Nielsen's envelope. Inside were copies of two cables. One was Kastrupbank's advice of the transfer from Zürich, the other was Tefler's confirmation. Drury studied them closely.

ZCH Rpt
17 Code/Clear
Kastrupbank
M.V. *Skagerrak*

> DDBBLBC/Carat Credit holder Amibank account BJO 1956 ten thousand U.S. dollars against satisfactory identification Bayer Kastrupbank

ZCH Rpt
17 Code/Clear
Kastrupbank
M.V. *Skagerrak*

M.V. *Skagerrak* Rpt
15 Code/Clear
Kastrupbank
Zürich

      DDBBLBC/Carat Holder Amibank account BJO
      1956 credited U.S. dollars ten thousand as per
      your today cable Tefler Kastrupbank

M.V. *Skagerrak* Rpt
15 Code/Clear
Kastrupbank
Zürich

EIGHT

It was hot in the radio room in spite of the air-conditioning. The door was locked, the counter shutter slightly raised. Nielsen had pulled the curtains across the portholes to shut out the sun. A small red light glowed in the semi-darkness. It was getting on for half-past four. Torpor seemed to have set in on board the *Skagerrak* except on the bridge and in the engine room. There had been nothing in or out since Tefler's cable to Zürich. Nielsen was sitting with his feet up on the desk, a shot-glass of Jim Beam whisky in his hand.

He was having some difficulty in getting his thinking clear. His whole world had changed in just a few hours. One minute he had been sitting there with a licence to coin money then suddenly he was dancing on air. The way things were going there was a strong possibility that he would spend the next few years of his life in the slammer. Munro's scheme might be foolproof for Munro but it offered nothing for anyone else. The only thing to do was slide off the coaster before it finally came to rest and run hard. Run just as fast as he could with whatever money he could lay his hands on. Montana had never seemed farther away.

The black phone buzzed and Nielsen reached for it. The purser was on the line. Nielsen had made half a dozen voyages with Voitek but their relationship had never gone beyond ship's business. The purser had a reputation for being a bit of a weirdo. Nielsen lowered his feet to the floor.

'What's on your mind?'

Voitek's voice was strangely conspiratorial. 'Are you alone?'

'You know damn well I'm alone,' Nielsen said bitterly. 'The kid's in hospital.'

'Can you step into my office for a moment. Now?'

Nielsen finished his drink and took his tunic from the back of the chair. It was no more than twenty feet to the purser's office but the staff captain required strict observance of the conventions. Nielsen locked the radio room behind him and crossed the Hall. Voitek was sitting alone in his office with the passenger list open in front of him. The entries gave the names, nationalities and passport numbers of all passengers.

'Shut the door and sit down!' Voitek instructed.

Nielsen pulled his chair away from the sunshine. There was a carpet bag on the floor by the wall. A musty smell came from it, camphor or incense. It was the second time that Nielsen had been in the purser's office and his curiosity was tinged with apprehension.

'You look terrible,' Voitek said suddenly. 'Like you were on horse-tranquillizers. Are you drinking again?'

'You're fucking right I'm drinking again,' Nielsen said savagely. 'Is life supposed to be so wonderful I should stop?'

'You ought to take more care of yourself,' said Voitek.

Nielsen looked at him warily. The purser's eyes were deep set and his nose sprang like a vulture's beak. There was a picture of a woman on the desk but you could never tell. Strange things happened on board ship.

'You haven't asked me here to talk about my health,' said Nielsen.

'No,' Voitek admitted and started at Nielsen thoughtfully.

Everything about the purser was dark. His eyes, his hair and his skin. The composite reminded Nielsen of a picture he had once seen, a sombre painting of a Pizarro priest burning an Indian who had refused the gospel message.

'You know I'm responsible for security aboard this ship?'

Voitek spoke with a sort of nervous concern as if worried at getting the wrong answer to his question.

'Sure,' Nielsen said guardedly. It was right enough technically, although the ultimate responsibility was the captain's. The way the conversation was going did nothing to reassure Nielsen.

Voitek leaned forward even further. 'This is strictly between you and me. I haven't been to the bridge with it yet.'

'No,' Nielsen said cautiously and wet his lips. There was a strong sense of unreality about the scene.

Voitek tapped on the passenger list with his forefinger. 'What I'm telling you here is in strict confidence, Ed.'

Nielsen blinked. Their relationship had always been formal. Suddenly it was 'Ed' and 'in confidence'. None of this was doing Nielsen any good. Frustration got the better of his judgement.

'Just what in hell are you talking about?' he demanded.

Voitek continued impassively. 'A leak at this stage could ruin the whole operation. The fact of the matter is this. I've got a strong hunch that we're carrying a couple of con men on board.'

'Con men?' Nielsen was croaking as though Voitek had just announced Christ's second coming. He was glad that he was already sitting down.

'That's right!' Voitek stabbed his forefinger as he talked. 'I cottoned onto this pair the moment they joined the cruise. I saw you talking to one of them yesterday.'

'Me?' Nielsen's responses were in danger of becoming stilted.

'A guy calling himself Jerry Jacumb,' said Voitek. 'In one-five-nine.'

'Oh *him*!' Nielsen tried for a look of innocent recollection. 'He was inquiring about cable rates to France.'

'Did you get an address?' Voitek asked quickly.

'He was just asking,' Nielsen said helplessly.

Voitek's voice rang with conviction. 'Never mind! The

guy's an operator. I spotted them both. His partner's up on the Bridge Deck too. A red-head sitting at the Captain's table last night. Believe me, Ed, you develop a nose for these things. I want this pair of bastards checked out.'

Things were breaking up fast around Nielsen. His mind ran a film. Cables speeding back and forth, the confrontation with Jacumb and Black. The three of them leaving the boat in cuffs. It looked as if he wasn't even going to get the chance to run.

'How can you be sure?' he asked in a voice he hardly recognized.

'Let's say that I can't be sure, but I'm certain.' Voitek showed yellow canine teeth. 'That's where you come in. I want you to send this cable for me.'

Nielsen read it through. The message was addressed to Sheriff Potocki, Dade County Sheriff's Department, Florida.

> Request background suspects Jerry Jacumb born Tacoma Washington January 7 1956 holder U.S. passport 198364 issued Los Angeles California stop Chester Black born Grand Rapids Michigan July 1 1952 holder U.S. passport 998124 issued New York New York stop
> Voitek Purser

'Potocki's a friend of mine,' said Voitek. 'League of Mary.' He looked as though he was about to tap his nose but restrained himself. 'Remember this is for our eyes only! We'll make these bastards sorry for the day they picked on the *Skagerrak*!'

Nielsen's eyes lifted from the typewritten sheet. 'What happens if these guys are clean?'

'Nothing.' Voitek grinned. 'That's the beauty of it, Ed. Only you and I will know anything about it. That's one of the reasons that I haven't gone to the bridge. I'm riding a hunch. If it's a bummer then we simply forget the whole thing. I'm trying to protect a man of the cloth here.'

Nielsen goggled. 'A man of the *cloth*?'

'A priest, a Jesuit father. The one who said mass on Sunday.'

'I'm an atheist,' said Nielsen. 'You mean a little fat guy, bald?'

'There's only one priest on the ship.' Voitek was obviously irritated. 'And this is no ordinary priest. The Jesuits are a sophisticated order. Were you in the services?'

'Korea.' It was all Nielsen intended to say about it.

'Well, the Jesuits are something like the Intelligence Corps. They're everywhere. The thing is, I happen to know that they're in the habit of handling large sums of money. Do you follow?'

'No,' said Nielsen.

'Moving this money from one country to another. Sometimes by hand.'

'You mean a sort of bagman?'

Voitek's brows bent in a frown. 'You don't describe a man of God as a bagman, Ed. I've got an idea that these crooks are into Father Mitrega and I intend to stop it. I've been watching them together.'

Nielsen gulped. 'It doesn't make sense.'

'It makes sense all right, buddy,' said Voitek. 'You'll see when we get the answer to this cable.'

Nielsen pushed his chair back. 'I'll get it off right away.'

Voitek offered his wolfish smile. 'I knew I could rely on you, Ed. And about the drinking. There's a guy I know in Tampa runs the local chapter of the A.A. He'd be real glad to see you.'

'Yep,' said Nielsen and escaped. Back in the radio room he called Jacumb but there was no reply. He deadlocked the door and closed the shutter entirely. He needed time to think. Jacumb and Black, whatever their real names were, might well be known to the police. He had no idea what was going on with this priest but one thing was certain. If Dade County Sheriff's Department showed a red light why then Voitek's siren would go off full blast. No, this was the moment to see all, hear all and do nothing to rock the boat.

His mind was now made up. Haiti was no place to run from. Another day and they'd be in San Juan. His cheque book and passport were down in his cabin. It might be better to leave the ship in uniform as though going ashore for a couple of hours. He could buy some duds and take the first plane out before all hell broke loose. There was no time to put together anything more ambitious. He tore the purser's cable into small pieces and sat down at the typewriter to compose a reply. He timed the message for some hours ahead. The end result was categorical.

Voitek Purser M.V. *Skagerrak*
Re your enquiry nothing known either suspect
Potocki Sheriff's Department

Nielsen licked an envelope and slipped the cable inside. It was just as well that Voitek hadn't decided to call his friend instead of cabling. Nielsen unlocked and made the office ready for business again. Voitek was standing at his door, looking across. Nielsen made a circle with his thumb and forefinger. It was after five and people were assembling for the first launch. The *Skagerrak* had dropped anchor in deep water between the capital and a peanut-shaped island called Ile-de-la-Gonâve. Perspective bent in the shimmering heat, the island shoreline appeared as though in a mirage. Far above the heat haze loomed a backdrop of steep green covered mountains and deeply gouged valleys.

Emily-May leaned over the rails. 'I spoke to Judy after lunch. She knows that something's going on.'

Drury removed a bug from his neck. 'I sort of slipped around the subject at lunch. We're having supper together. It's a prospect that I don't exactly relish.'

The bugs had appeared from the mainland along with a pungent smell of rotting vegetation. They were large, black and fearless, though apparently without stings. They crawled on the rails and the ventilators, clustering on the hot bright brass. Emily-May brushed a couple from her arm. She was looking relaxed in a tan coloured dress and a large floppy hat.

'I'm supposed to be seeing her afterwards. She may not want to talk to me by then.'

'Jesus Christ,' he said heavily.

She turned towards him, her eyes full of sympathy. 'You have to do it, Phil, it's important for everyone. You're going to have to tell her about Mark and you're going to have to tell her about me.'

'Brilliant,' he said unhappily. 'I drop a ton of bricks on her and she winds up believing in nobody.'

'Rubbish!' She touched his sleeve with her hand. 'Play it by ear. You've got one thing going for you, Phil. That girl loves you very much. It'll take a lot of destroying.'

He was suddenly sick of the conversation. A white launch flying the Haitian naval standard above the Danish-Lloyd house flag had appeared through the haze. They pushed through a thicket of cameras and binoculars to where Judy was waiting at the bottom of the stairs.

Judy's eyes were curious. 'Where have you two been hiding? I've been looking for you everywhere.'

He took her arm, wondering if she resented him being with Emily-May. The thought was ironical. He helped them both down the gangway. Deckhands were steadying the launch with ropes. The black crew below moved with lazy efficiency. Not a movement was made with extravagance of effort. A barefooted sailor wearing a Napoleonic uniform handed down each passenger with a show of teeth and melodious greeting.

''soir, 'sieurs, 'dames!'

They seated themselves in the bows. Shoals of small brilliantly coloured fish nuzzled the side of the launch, darting away as the shadow of Emily-May's hat disturbed the pattern of light. Drury could see Russell up on the Bridge Deck standing with Jacumb. A flash of white behind them drew Drury's attention. He borrowed a neighbour's binoculars. The purser's face came into focus. His interest

seemed to be centered on Russell and Jacumb. Drury
returned the binoculars. The launch cast off to a mild
cheer from those left behind. The heat haze dissolved as
they neared the shore and the water grew progressively
dirtier. Close to the wharf, dead dogs and cats, obscenely
swollen and eyeless, floated belly-up among rotting fruit,
broken crates and plastic containers. The launch went into
reverse, backing in the scummy water until its side
bumped against the truck tyres that served as fenders. An
enormous shed extended two hundred yards along the
stone-built wharf. Barricades had been placed so that
disembarking passengers were led into the customs shed.
The barefooted bosun handed Emily-May and Judy from
the launch with old world courtesy. Drury followed them
into the lofty building. The odour of spices compounded
with the stench of rotting vegetation. The ends of the shed
were open to what small breezes blew. The roof and girders
were iron but in spite of this it was cool inside. Birds used
the stanchions as perches, hawking the bugs that flew and
crawled below. Two long trestle tables stood under a sign
proclaiming *Duvalier President Pour La Vie*. The black
customs officials wore baggy cotton uniforms and soiled
white gloves. The only policeman in sight was an enormous man built on the lines of a Japanese wrestler. He was
sitting on a chair near the exit, smoking a large cigar and
wearing dark glasses. The handle of his .45 was made of
mother-of-pearl, the peak of his cap heavily decorated
with gold braid. Beyond him was a vista of black faces, of
flowers and fruit piled high in profusion. The women
selling them wore dresses that reached to the ground, their
hair tied in magnificent turbans. Behind them was a line
of ancient taxis.

The passengers started filing past the customs officers
who stood behind the tables. None carried more than a
handbag or camera. The officials glanced at each passport
perfunctorily, stamped it and issued a card redeemable
upon leaving at the cost of two dollars. Drury and the two
women walked out into hot oppressive sunshine. Emac-

iated dogs lay in what shade they could find. Blind men led by urchins bawled monotonously. A beggar without arms or legs propelled himself face down, his stumps pushing from a wooden trolley. In the middle of all this, a giant skeletal figure in a loincloth slowly revolved in the dust, piercing his body with hatpins.

Squashed mangoes made the ground slippery and the air reeked with the cloying scent of red jasmine. A policeman lifted a rope. A swarm of touts and peddlers burst out brandishing cards and boards bearing the names of hotels and restaurants. Others carried baskets filled with giant conch shells, quartz watches and radios from Taiwan. Drury used his bulk to clear a passage for Emily-May and Judy, slowly forcing his way towards the line of taxis. These were curiously adorned with strings of rosary beads, pictures of saints and rag dolls dangling from rearview mirrors and dashboards. Some of the cars had religious motifs painted on the bodywork. Drury halted at a pre-war Cadillac, waxed and polished to a mirrorlike surface. A card was propped on the fender: *Good Driver Sweet Talker English.*

The chauffeur was magnificent in a Rastifarian robe and fez. Emily-May shrugged. 'He looks like a gentle soul.'

Drury opened the rear door and the two women got in. The driver continued to beam.

'Seven-thirty,' Drury said to his daughter. 'The bar of the Hotel Oluffson.' He placed a ten dollar bill in the driver's ready palm. 'Drive these ladies to the Iron Market and take good care of them.'

The Rastifarian's smile widened. 'Have no fear, Monsieur. I am best driver in all Haiti with diploma. I tell my cousin he take care of ladies in Iron Market. No whistle. No hankypanky.' He went through a pinching motion with thumb and forefinger.

Emily-May and Judy were fending off flies with their hands. 'Offer half whatever they ask,' advised Drury, 'and walk away at least once. They'll expect it.'

The cab drove off, the Rastifarian's thumb bearing down

on the horn button, scattering everything in front of him. An urchin sidled up to Drury. His ebony face was spattered with dried water-melon seeds and his front teeth were missing.

'Me Jean-Baptiste. You want dope I got you want girl I got!'

'Ecoute,' said Drury sternly. '*Tu vas me trouver une agence de voyages, tu comprends?*' He held up a dollar bill. It was better to give this ten-year-old racketeer money and have him fend off the rest of the operators.

The urchin's respect increased visibly at the sound of Drury's French. He picked up a stout length of wood and gave a gap-toothed grin. '*Suis-moi, Papa!*' He marched along in front of Drury, stave shouldered like a rifle.

The traffic was wild and undisciplined. Cyclists were weaving their shaky ways through American and Japanese pick-ups equipped with hard seats and burlap awnings. None of the vehicles looked less than fifteen years old. People hunkered down on the kerb. Dogs, children, the aged and the afflicted crossed the street at random. The result added to the general noise and disorder. Drury's pilot led him into a network of steep streets where whitewashed buildings leaned and bulged, their precarious balconies hung with hibiscus and jasmine. The shops below were stuffed with primitive paintings, the flotsam of the city and the junk from every Caribbean free port. A corner building squatted above a pavement cafe. Next to it was a shop with a modern front. The urchin whirled, stamped his bare feet and presented arms with his stick. Then he stuck out his hand with a splendid grin.

'*Voilà, mon Papa!*'

Drury gave him the dollar bill and walked into the cool of the *Agence France*. Two enormous ceiling fans the size of aeroplane propellors were slowly revolving, lifting the papers on the tables and desks. The counter was made from solid mahogany. A mulatto wearing a pink shirt and a powdering of what looked like gold dust on his cheekbones drifted across, looking at Drury with sad eyes. Drury spent the next twenty minutes going through flight schedules with the clerk. He left the travel agency carrying four tickets in his pocket. Three of them were certainly going to be used. The fourth he was not yet sure about.

Benjy Field joined the queue for the second launch. He had watched the Canadian and the two women go ashore on the first trip. Sheldon and the priest, zipped together as usual now, would be following. Benjy braced himself against the wheelhouse as the launch pulled away. He gaped, dragging salt air into his lungs then closed his mouth suddenly, aware that he was being watched. He turned his head slowly. The purser was leaning against the rails a few feet away. The launch chugged on through the haze. Benjy viewed the approaching shoreline with some misgiving. His impressions of Haiti had been formed by magazines read at his dentist and old newsreels. The first black republic, voodoo and Tonton Macoutes, negro heavies wearing two-tone shoes and carrying Lugers that would take your head off at twenty paces.

The launch glided at half speed through scummy water towards what looked like a customs shed. Benjy was among the first to land. He walked across the concrete floor to the waiting officials. He had his phoney passport stamped by a man with eyes like chestnuts swimming in glycerine. The man gave him a card and waved him on towards the exit. Outside was pandemonium. Benjy shoved his way through the ranks of pimps, beggars and flower sellers to the line of waiting taxis. He yanked open the door of an ancient Dodge. The leather seat was patched and exuded a strong feral smell.

'Pétionville!' said Benjy. 'La Guingette.'

The chauffeur nodded. He was wearing a t-shirt and a visored cap bearing the insignia of the United States Navy. A statue of a black Virgin Mary was taped on the partition with a vase of plastic roses under it. The Dodge moved off with whining transmission, threading its way through donkeys laden down with yams and bananas, pick-up trucks that seemed to be serving as buses. Beggars and children spilled out from the pavements. Overhead were faded streamers advertising forgotten festivals. Benjy thumbed a Lucky from the packet and leaned forward to light it. As the match flared, his eyes caught the driver's rearview mirror. A green taxi was following some twenty yards behind, the purser in the back doing his best to make himself inconspicuous.

Benjy's reaction was instinctive. 'Take a left!' he bawled. The driver kept going. 'Gauche!' yelled Benjy, salvaging the word from French 1. He emphasized the direction with a swing of his hand.

The car swayed, springs complaining as the vehicle bucked its way over the potholes in the rising ground. Benjy grabbed the leather loop by the window, noticing for the first time that the tip of the driver's left ear was missing. Benjy bounced high, striving for the French word for slow but his memory was exhausted. The hill grew steeper, the road narrower. The speed and jolting of the cab gave Benjy angled shots of the scene outside. Washing hanging from a peeling house front, a woman at a window breast feeding a baby, a caged fighting cock on a balcony.

He thrust his arm over the driver's shoulder and indicated another turn. The car lurched, chassis sagging, then swerved again. Benjy looked back. The green Ford was no longer there. It *had* to be coincidence, there was no other logical explanation. The address he had given the driver was one of five supplied by Lansky. Lansky was supposed to have the best contacts in the Caribbean. Like everything else that he supplied, you paid through the nose for it but the goods were reliable. The Dodge turned onto a strip of hardtop laid along the dried-up bed of a river. Oleander trees grew along the rock-scabbed sides of the *arroyo*. A man wearing a ragged straw hat was tilling a patch of dirt with the aid of a donkey the size of a large dog. The *arroyo* debouched onto a bluff, set with dusty palm trees. Port-au-Prince lay a thousand feet below. A breeze was blowing and it was several degrees cooler up here. Whitewashed hovels clustered round a small square where an iron statue of Toussaint l'Ouverture stood in a blocked fountain overgrown by weeds. Nothing else moved except the dust that rose and settled in the wake of the taxi. The chauffeur turned through a pair of sagging gates onto a dirt driveway that wound through the palms. Coloured lights were strung through the branches and on a faded banner was written *A La Guingette Rien Que Les Vedettes.*

Torm posters advertised third rate French *chanteuses*, Cuban bands and limbo dancers. The dirt road ended in front of a stonebuilt two storey mansion with a deep porch covered in bougainvillaea and wrought iron balconies. The driver turned, his English suddenly working.

'Ten dollars!'

Benjy gave him the money and walked towards the open front door. The lofty hall was dim, the passage of light obstructed by the greenery that trailed across the windows. Benjy raised his voice.

'Is there anyone around?'

No one answered. Benjy moved forward into the shadows. A monkey chained to a pole swung by its tail, chattering as Benjy approached. A conservatory filled with tropical plants and Victorian wickerwork led to a frame extension. Benjy could see through to a dance floor, a stage and tables. He turned sharply, hearing a noise behind him. A black woman with white springy hair and enormous breasts was standing in a doorway watching. Benjy smiled.

'Bishirgian?'

She backed off, her face a mahogany mask. The door closed behind her. Benjy called again.

'Is anyone home? Mister Bishirgian?'

His voice echoed in the gallery surrounding the hall. An iron stairway led up to the second storey. Benjy lit a cigarette, keeping his distance from the monkey. The door opened suddenly. The man who emerged was white and quite old. He walked towards Benjy, supporting his weight on a cane with a rhinoceros horn handle. He was wearing a suit of blue tussore silk and black dancing pumps.

'Who are you?' he demanded. 'What do you want?'

Benjy felt in his pocket. 'Mister Bishirgian?'

The old man's eyes were clear and steady, younger than the rest of his face. 'I am Bishirgian.'

Benjy handed him the sealed envelope. 'Lansky sent me.'

Bishirgian used his thumbnail to rip open the envelope and extracted the note inside. He held the envelope to the light, making sure that nothing had been left inside then put it away in his pocket. He read Lansky's note through twice.

'You are Benjy Field?' he asked, looking up.

Benjy nodded.

'Are you Jewish?'

The last time Benjy had thought of himself as being Jewish had been at his *barmitzvah* party.

'Right.'

'Good,' said Bishirgian. 'I like Jews, come!'

Leaning heavily on his cane, he led the way into the conservatory. They seated themselves at a wicker table. Bishirgian produced a small silver bell from his pocket and rang it. The old negress appeared, carrying a tray set with a bottle of white rum, fresh limes, ice and glasses. There was a bowl containing sugar. She put down the tray and waddled away.

Bishirgian inclined his head. 'You like Daiquiris or you prefer something else?'

'The way you're going to fix them I like Daiquiris,' said Benjy. There was a tiny grotto where ferns waved in falling water and exotic flowers bloomed in conch shells. Benjy turned away hurriedly as he saw the snake's body writhe along the dead bough.

Bishirgian showed a mouthful of ancient teeth. '*Shalom aleikum!*'

Benjy lifted the chilled glass. '*Mazeltov!*'

Bishirgian smacked his lips like a gorilla. 'So Lansky is well.'

'Blooming like a rose,' said Benjy. Lansky weighed two hundred and eighty pounds and was popularly known as 'meathead'.

Bishirgian cackled appreciation. 'You have a sense of humour, Benjy. Now how can I help you?'

Benjy's face sobered. He had a secret contempt for people like this man and Lansky. Their time had long gone, but they refused to accept it, blocking the way for younger men with new ideas.

'I need a couple of things.'

Bishirgian set his glass down carefully and waved away a fly. 'You are a passenger on the cruise ship?'

'That's right,' said Benjy.

'And working?' Bishirgian's eyes were bright. 'Lansky gives you a good reputation.'

'I need a gun,' said Benjy. 'A small gun that I can have in my pocket without it being noticed.'

'This is no problem,' said the old man. 'I will take you into the city and you can make your own choice.'

The kicker in the Daiquiri had just reached Benjy's nervous system. 'Do you know a guy in San Juan called Spinoza?'

'Abel Spinoza?'

'That's the guy.'

'Abel is an old friend of mine.'

Benjy nodded. Spinoza was another of the names on Lansky's list. 'I want you to call him for me tonight. Tell him I need a plane with room for two passengers. I want it gassed up and ready to go any time after three o'clock tomorrow afternoon. And tell him we don't want to go through any kind of police or passport check. You follow?'

Bishirgian's eyes hooded like a lizard's. He looked as though many such requests had been made to him before.

'You say you need space for *two* passengers?'

'My brother,' said Benjy. 'He's Jewish too.'

They stared at one another for the space of a thought or two and then Bishirgian smiled. 'And what will be the destination of this plane?'

'We'll get to that later,' said Benjy. These old-timers asked too many questions.

Bishirgian ran a veined hand down his jawline. 'What you are asking for will require preparation. Abel Spinoza will insist on knowing your destination.'

The stink of the monkey was all-pervading in spite of the heavily scented flowers.

'Guadaloupe,' Benjy said reluctantly. 'You can tell him that we want to be put down in a field somewhere with transport waiting to take us into Pointe-à-Pitre airfield.' He had checked it out. Air Canada jetted non-stop to Montreal, Air France to Paris and there were flights to the States.

Bishirgian twisted a scarab ring on his finger. 'All this will cost money, Benjy.' His voice was very sad.

'The money will be there,' Benjy said with easy assurance.

Bishirgian pushed himself up onto his cane. 'I think it will be better if you talk to Abel yourself.'

Benjy followed the old man into an office decorated with pictures of forgotten French actresses. Bishirgian lifted the phone and dialled, leaving the receiver lying on the desk. The ringing tone was loud. Suddenly it stopped. Bishirgian picked up the handset.

'Abel? Nahum Bishirgian. Yes, I am well, praise be to God! I have someone here who wishes to speak to you, a friend of Lansky's.' He passed the phone to Benjy and nodded encouragingly. Benjy explained his needs.

Spinoza had a strong Brooklyn accent and wasted no time. 'Three o'clock tomorrow you say?'

'Any time after three, not before.'

'That gives me less than a day.'

'We won't be carrying baggage,' said Benjy. 'Nothing but what's in our pockets.'

'Make sure there's money in 'em,' said Spinoza. Benjy could hear no joke in the voice. 'This is going to cost you ten grand, cake on the line.'

'It'll be there.'

'OK. So what time do you dock?'

'We're scheduled in at eleven.'

'Do you know San Juan?'

'Not the first thing.'

'I'll send a cab to the pier. Come straight out to the house. I'll be waiting for you.'

Benjy put the phone down, his voice curious. 'That was quick.'

Bishirgian spread his hands. 'It's easier to call San Juan than Port-au-Prince. Now if you are willing, my driver will take us down to the city and you can select the weapon of your preference.' He made it sound like the preliminary to a duel.

Benjy was still inquisitive. 'What kind of a business do you run here? Lansky said it was a night club but the only person I've seen is the old coon who brought us the drinks.'

'My wife,' said Bishirgian. He touched a button on the floor with his foot. 'We keep late hours in Haiti. The club opens at midnight. Some of my people live down below, some in the village. My wife and I do not care for strangers about the house.'

A 1950 front wheel drive Citroën was waiting out front, as shiny and black as a roach. A middle-aged man with faulty pigmentation and a distinct resemblance to Bishirgian whipped off his chauffeur's cap as they approached. He opened the rear door and Bishirgian climbed in first. The route the driver took was circuitous but the road surface was better. He stopped the Citroën outside a cigar store on the Rue de la Revolution. Women were sitting in the window, hand-rolling leaf tobacco. Others were packing the cigars into boxes. None of the women as much as looked up as Bishirgian's cane tapped across the floor.

Bishirgian opened a door leading to a small paved yard

with a hibiscus tree growing in the middle. A large dark
man was swinging in a hammock ten feet up in the air. He
was smoking a fat joint and opened his eyes in lazy
recognition.

Bishirgian sat on a bench covered with bird droppings.
'*Bonjour*, Hippolyte! Is your mind clear today?'

Like Bishirgian, Hippolyte spoke in *patois*. 'My mind is
clear, Papa Bishirgian.' He removed the joint from his
mouth, displaying teeth heavily inlaid with gold.

'Weapons,' said Bishirgian, poking his cane through the
bars of a cage. A fighting cock flew at the ferrule. 'A
hand-gun.'

Hippolyte drew the acrid smoke deep into his lungs and
held it there before exhaling. 'I am a timorous man, Papa
Bishirgian. The streets have ears and the doorways eyes.'

Bishirgian pointed his cane at Benjy. 'This is a friend, a
man with secret knowledge, but to fulfill it he needs a gun
small enough to be concealed about his person.'

The seeds popped in Hippolyte's joint. 'A man with
secret knowledge, aieee! In Haiti there is much secret
knowledge. I wonder if he has ever heard of it?'

'This is secret knowledge of a superior kind,' said
Bishirgian. 'He is able to make men disappear.'

'Ah,' said Hippolyte, much impressed.

Bishirgian showed his horse teeth in a gentle smile.
'Show me, Hippolyte.'

The big man rolled out of his hammock, maintaining his
body in a horizontal position until the last possible
moment. Then his feet flashed out and found the ground.
He grinned, plainly pleased with his performance, and
opened a door in the stonework. Lizards ran from the
movement of his hand. A young woman in the room inside
moved with the speed and grace of a puma, snatching up
something and vanishing silently. The room was oppressively furnished with a mahogany table and chairs. The legs
were set in tin bowls full of kerosene. There was a great
deal of tasselled red velvet, a coloured print of the Last
Supper next to a fearsome portrait of Baron Samedi. A

photograph of President Duvalier rested on top of the refrigerator. The scream of a baby outside mingled with the squawking of the fighting cock. Hippolyte opened the refrigerator, smiling indulgently as he pulled out the deep vegetable tray. He placed this on the red velvet table-cloth, removed the lid and whipped out a police special .38. He checked the loaded clip and sighted the gun at Benjy.

Benjy was outraged. 'What's he trying to do?' he yelled in English. 'Does he want to get us all killed?'

'He is showing off,' said Bishirgian and peeked into the vegetable tray. 'Do you see anything here that you like? If not we will go somewhere else.'

Hippolyte's hand moved quickly. When he opened it, a tiny gun with a two inch barrel nestled in his pink palm. His melodious voice was plainly singing the weapons' praises. Bishirgian interpreted.

'He says that it is made in Taipei and fires five shots. He also says that it will destroy your testicles at ten paces. The price is two hundred United States dollars.'

Benjy hefted the miniature gun. It was hand-forged of blued steel and small enough to fit in the king size cigarette pack he had in his pocket. Five tiny shells loaded into a minute clip.

Bishirgian's voice grated. 'He says that this is a weapon fit for a wizard.'

'I'll take it.' Benjy gave the Negro two hundred-dollar bills. A thought struck him. 'This is a custom-made gun. What about shells?'

Bishirgian interpreted again and Hippolyte produced a small box. 'A present,' Bishirgian explained. 'He wishes for your blessing and expresses the wish that the testicles you remove will be those of your enemies.'

'He's got a hangup on balls,' said Benjy, 'but tell him I bless him.'

They walked out through the cigar store. The Citroën was waiting. Bishirgian offered his veined hand. It was dry and warm like the skin of a bird.

'Goodbye, my young friend. What was it again "blooming like a rose"? I shall remember. I am glad to have been
of some service.'

Benjy watched the sleek old car corner as if on tracks.
He stood in the doorway, emptied the pack of Luckys and
put the small gun inside. Things had gone even better than
he had expected.

Drury climbed up steps made slippery by squashed and
rotting fruit. Beggars infested with sores were sprawling
against yellowed walls that stank like latrines. Brown and
white goats browsed among the rubble where primitive
shacks had once stood. The air in the open market was
oppressively still, the sun partially obscured by a black-
bellied cloud that threatened a tropical rainstorm. Drury
had seen the souks of North Africa but nothing that
matched the surrounding squalor and misery. The slow-
moving crowd saw it all with indifference if not with
apathy. The condition was endemic like syphilis or
malaria. Home-made booths had been constructed from
whatever material came to hand, branches pulled from the
cane brakes and palm trees, flattened out cans and packing
crates. Vendors sat or squatted, offering peanuts, women's
underwear, primitive paintings of tigers and giraffes. A
man in a loin-cloth was fashioning clogs from old rubber
tyres.

Drury turned right into a street hung with tattered flags.
A shop selling luggage offered sets of matching bags made
in South Korea. One bag fitted inside another for ease of
storage. Drury made his purchase and carried it out
wrapped in brown paper. It was almost seven-thirty when
he walked into the hotel. From the outside, the overgrown
mansion looked like the product of some troubled imagination, a Charles Addams drawing brought to life. It was
another world entirely once in the air-conditioned lobby.
Black and white guests mingled freely, the Haitians
colourfully dressed and flamboyant. Parisian accents
outnumbered the sound of *patois*. Drury left his parcel in

the cloakroom and walked across the lobby to a bar where a coffee coloured pianist was playing soulfully. Judy was sitting alone, her head bent, poring over her crossword puzzle. He came up quietly and kissed the back of her neck. She whirled, colour flaming in her face.

'God! I wish you wouldn't do that. You know how much I hate it!'

He hoisted himself onto the stool beside her and signalled the barman. The house lights flickered as he ordered. A clap of thunder seemed to lift the roof. The black cloud overhead fired rain like a water-gun, bombarding the windows and breaking down the orange flowers of the giant bucare trees outside. Drury's drink came made with Barbancourt rum, exotic in taste and yet not cloying. He put his glass down.

'What have you done with Emily-May?'

She folded her newspaper. 'She went to the Canadian Consulate. We just about walked our legs off, pursued by nine hundred beggars. The Museum of Art put the finishing touches. These were the only things that I saw worth buying.' She thrust out a suntanned leg, displaying gold-strapped sandals.

'Cute,' he said. 'They go with your dress.'

The rain had stopped as suddenly as it had begun. The tiled garden paths were steaming.

Judy turned. 'I told Emily-May to come at nine o'clock. She'll have eaten. I thought it would give us time to talk.'

He nodded and placed a bill on the bar, leaving the rest of his drink. The dreaded moment was approaching. The downpour had left the dining verandah blissfully fresh, evoking the heady scent of flowers. The heat haze had been washed away by the rain leaving a distant view of the *Skagerrak* riding out in the harbour.

No one else was eating as yet. They chose Creole-style food, lobster meat sautéd in butter then flamed in rum. It was served with fried plantains and brown rice. Judy reached for the wine list and ordered a bottle of Krug '72.

'I'm paying for this,' she said firmly and leaned across the table, taking one of Drury's hands in her own. 'Is it really going to be so bad, this terrible secret?'

The sweetness in her voice brought a lump to his throat. He found it hard to get rid of. She tugged at his fingers very gently. 'Papa! Come *on* now! I can't bear to see you like this.'

He shook his head ruefully. 'I wish to God . . .'

She dropped his hand. 'OK, then we'll do it this way. First we eat and then drink and then we talk. Agreed?'

He nodded, glad of the respite. Her warmth and sympathy only made things worse. They ended their meal with goat's cheese and spiced peanut butter. He drank the last of the champagne and produced his cigar case.

'Let's go out in the garden.'

She paid the bill, declining the offer of coffee. She angled the chair so that she could see his face. They were sitting twenty yards away from the verandah and there was no one in the garden but themselves. He lit her cigarette.

'Right,' she said, exhaling. 'Talk away.'

He found it hard to begin. The opening speech he had planned was forgotten and his words came in an ugly rush. 'Orbec was started with money that I stole. I'm a thief, Judy.'

A lizard ran out of its crack in the stone and stood still. Judy's pose was equally quiet.

'Well, come on,' he challenged. Her silence made his voice almost combative. 'Aren't you going to say something?'

She turned her head slowly, looking at him through the smoke from her cigarette.

'There's nothing to say. I've known that ever since I was sixteen. Mama told me the whole story.'

'Jesus *Christ*!' The news shocked him profoundly. It had been hard enough for Helen to accept what had happened. Never would he have suspected that she would have talked to their daughter about it.

'Why not?' Judy asked simply. 'It was much easier for

Mama to explain than for you. In any case, I don't think you'd have been able to make me understand, not at that age anyway. Mama could.'

It should have been easier now to go on, but it wasn't. He drew deep on his cigar.

'That isn't all,' he said punishing himself. 'It gets better. All that stuff in London about investing the money from your mother's insurance. Bullshit, every single word of it. There *is* no insurance money. It went like everything else.'

She smiled, strangely unmoved. 'I guessed that was what had happened. A con man you may have been but you can't con me. So what? I keep telling you this, I have more than enough for both of us.'

He shook his head, staring past her into the steaming bushes. Two down and one to go. 'You don't understand, honey. I'm *still* a thief. Right now I'm planning to rob a bank.'

The involuntary gesture took her fingers to her throat. 'You have to be kidding!'

He let his breath go, seeing the apprehension in her eyes. 'I'm afraid not, Judy. This is something I have to do.'

'I don't *believe* it,' she said. 'Robbing a bank is something that you have to do?'

He shook his head sadly. 'I knew it would be no good.'

'It *can't* be good if you don't explain,' she said. Spirit was back in her manner and her eyes were lively. 'I want to know *why* you have to do it! Come on now, Papa. *Explain!* No more lies between us, just the truth, promise?'

'I promise,' he said, looking down at the ash on the end of his cigar. His voice flat and emotionless, he told her what was happening, not sparing himself.

She lifted her head. 'And you've known Emily-May and Russell for all these years. Did Mama know them?'

He nodded. 'She met them once in Acapulco, years ago. OK, now you know the worst. The rest is up to you. You have to make a choice. Whatever it is, sweetheart, I'll understand.'

A bird flew from a branch overhead, dislodging drops of rain. She brushed them off her forearm, still looking at her father.

'But *why*? That's what I don't get. It would help if I knew. You mean Emily-May's a fraud as well, a crook?'

'Emily-May's a woman of sixty odd with a distinguished career as a writer,' he said. 'And for half of those sixty years, she's been in love with the same man. No, she's no fraud.'

Judy frowned. 'OK, OK! But *you*, Papa! It isn't as if you needed this money.'

He lifted his shoulders and let them fall. How to explain to girl like Judy? How to explain the reluctance to be a charge on anyone, the satisfaction of getting an old friend back on the rails, the sheer joy of the rush of adrenalin in face of danger?

He grinned. 'In any case these kids deserve to be taught a lesson.'

'Ridiculous!' she burst out. 'How much of this stuff do you expect me to take? Do you mean to tell me that you think of yourself as some kind of avenging angel?'

'No,' he admitted. 'Maybe it's greed. Maybe it's a little of everything. I only know that I have to do it.'

'Did you ever go to jail?' she asked suddenly.

'Nope,' he said shortly and smiled. 'I always had the wind behind me.'

'Well, I guess that's something.' She managed the glow of an answering smile. 'I'm not too sure that I know what to say, Papa. I never handled anything quite like this before.'

He deliberately shut out all feeling from his voice. 'You do what you feel to be right, honey. Go right out to the airport tomorrow and leave. I'll understand.'

'That's what worries me,' she said, her face anxious. 'I go. What happens to you?'

He spread his hands. 'I have to stay. It's my last chance. It's Mark's last chance.'

'And *Emily-May's* last chance?' The way she said it made it sound ridiculous.

'In a weird kind of way, maybe yes,' he replied.

She made a noise of irritation. 'You're really pulling out all the stops, deliberately doing your best to turn me against you. The cold-hearted villain, deaf to any appeal. Well, it just won't work. We're the same flesh and blood. Remember what you used to tell me: families and friends stick together, this is the way to survive in the jungle! I'm not running out on you now, Papa. I'd sooner have you where I can see you and worry, than worry and not know what's happening.'

His whole body flooded with relief. 'I can say that I'm sorry, but I can't feel ashamed.'

'I don't want either,' she said quickly. She felt in her bag for her lipstick. 'Emily-May's standing on the steps.'

They walked up the path to the verandah. Emily-May inspected both their faces.

'You've told her?' she asked Drury.

Judy answered for him. 'He's told me.'

Drury walked across the lobby to the cloakroom. 'So?' Emily-May asked quietly.

Judy looked the older woman straight in the eye. 'I guess I ought to despise you. Don't get me wrong – for making a fool of me! But it's strange, I don't. You just happen to love that odd little man and I love my father. It shouldn't, but somehow that makes everything all right. And there's something that I could never forget. My father gave me a home where growing up and being a child was all happiness.'

Emily-May's look was wise. 'Your father always did what had to be done. There's a good word for that – integrity. He's got more of that than any other man that I know.'

Judy's mouth trembled as though she was close to tears. Emily-May took her arm and held it tight.

'Don't let him see.'

Judy shook her head furiously. 'Don't worry. I want him

where I know what's happening, Emily-May. I couldn't bear the uncertainty. You're a woman, you can understand that.'

Emily-May squeezed Judy's arm. 'I understand only too well, honey. And that little bugger of mine knows it, too. They need us, I guess. And that's about all there is to it!'

Gaunt cats and dogs were prowling among the refuse that littered the front of the customs shed. The crowds had vanished. A couple of bored officials were processing passengers returning to the *Skagerrak*. Drury surrendered the tourist cards and six dollars. The official waved the trio on, indifferent to the package that Drury was carrying. They went on through to the waiting launch. The *Skagerrak* was ablaze with lights, three-quarters of a mile away. Drury saw the ship with a feeling of anti-climax. The worst was over and all his fears had been groundless. Nothing had changed between Judy and him.

There were no tickets for the return journey. It was a case of first come, first served. The bosun handed the women aboard, flashing his smile. A bell rang and the launch backed off. The shoreline gradually receded. Night had cleansed the water, hiding the flotsam the small boat left in its wake. Bright stars overhead were pasted against an indigo sky. They climbed the gangway to the Main Deck. The casino and disco were open and the corridors echoed with the beat of heavy rock.

Drury looked at the two women. 'How about a nightcap?'

Judy shook her head. 'I'm going to fold. I'm beat.'

Drury walked her across to the lifts. The gate opened and he drew her close. 'Sleep tight, honey.' He wanted to say so much more, but it was all he could risk.

She nodded. 'You too.'

'And thanks for everything.' This much he had to say.

Her voice barely reached him. 'That's the silliest thing I've heard today.' Her eyes stayed with him as the gate closed.

He found Emily-May waiting where he had left her. They walked out on deck. The ship was rocking slightly, the sound from the disco blending with the grumble of the donkey-engine.

'I'm going to give you a piece of advice,' Emily-May said quietly. 'Don't lean on that girl. She's just made one helluva decision.'

Her face was in shadow but her tone of voice left no doubt about her sincerity.

'I don't lean on people, least of all Judy,' he answered.

She moved into the light deliberately. 'You don't know *what* you do, Phil Drury. The worst kind of leaner is the guy who doesn't think that he's one.'

A sense of injustice sharpened his tone. 'If we're still on the subject of Judy, I say bullshit! If anything the boot's on the other foot.'

'Not any more it isn't,' she said and leaned back against the rails. 'You want to change the subject?'

He looked at her steadily for a moment then smiled. 'Sure. Let's talk business.'

'What are you going to do with that child?' she demanded.

'Hang on,' he said. 'I thought you wanted to change the subject.'

She corrected his statement. 'Wrong! I asked if *you* wanted to?'

'OK,' he said. 'But will you believe me if I tell you?'

'I always believe what you tell me,' she answered quietly.

'Which is more than I can say for most people.'

He lit her cigarette and slipped her lighter back in her bag. 'That child is a grown woman who happened to marry a brute. I'm going to try to repair the harm that he did and the harm that I've done.'

'Brave words,' she said. 'Just be sure that you tread lightly.'

But the glance she shot at him could have come in a box

lined with black velvet. 'You're OK, Phil Drury. Unroll the scenario.'

'It'll work,' he promised when he had done. 'The essence is timing. Do you think you can handle your end?'

'With one hand tied behind my back,' she said coolly. 'And where's Judy going to be while all this is happening?'

'Waiting out at the airport.'

'You're wrong,' she argued. 'This girl has made her choice. She'll want to play a full part. We're not talking about moral issues any more. These have already been decided. She's one of us, Phil. Part of a team. And don't laugh!'

'I'm not laughing,' he said, 'and I guess you're right.'

The launch had made its last run and was on its way to the shore. The tempo of the donkey-engine increased as the deckhands made the *Skagerrak* ready for sailing.

'I'll have to risk talking to Mark,' he said. 'I can't trust the phone.'

She rose and flicked her cigarette end over the side. 'Good night, old buddy,' she said quietly.

He used the phone in the Terrace Bar to call Russell's cabin. 'Get yourself up to the big observation deck and make sure that nobody's on your tail.'

A rattle of chains followed the chugging of the donkey-engine and the anchor began to rise slowly. Drury took the lift up to his deck and walked on past his cabin. A storm door with a heavy glass panel sealed off the corridor. Drury lifted the lever and stepped out into the railed off space immediately above the wheelhouse. Bells below were ringing signals to the engine room. The ship moved forward slowly, waves of white water appearing as it gathered momentum, leaving the lights of Port-au-Prince astern. He had left the storm door ajar and could hear the clang of the lift cage closing. Seconds later Russell appeared, rolling a little as he walked forward. He pulled the heavy door shut after him. His collar was stained with wine. His hand poked out of his shirt sleeve as his arm lifted.

'Russell's dread curse strikes again.'

Drury caught hold of him. 'Are you drunk or what?'

Russell hiccoughed. 'They plied me with liquor, a man of God!'

'You bastard!' said Drury, the scene running through his head. He was going to have to get this drunk into a bath and get a gallon of coffee inside him.

'Sucker!' said Russell, his face changing to one enormous grin, the drunkenness gone. 'They've gone for it, kid, hook, line and sinker!'

The lights of Haiti were fading fast with the *Skagerrak* heading out to sea in the general direction of Puerto Rico.

'What exactly have they told you to do?' asked Drury.

Russell's voice dripped self-satisfaction. 'They gave me the business about this asshole Black defrauding the Internal Revenue by declaring a charitable bequest for five hundred grand and glomming back four hundred. I brought up the moral issues involved, a man of the cloth and so forth.'

'Of course.' Drury had seen Russell working at the top of his form, the sandbag concealed in the jester's balloon.

Russell winked. 'But the church's wisdom is all-embracing. I'm taking the one hundred big ones for the Mary-mount Building Fund. *Mea culpa, mea culpa, mea maxima culpa.*'

'Yeah,' said Drury, leaning over the rails. No cloud obscured the face of the moon and its reflection in the water was perfect. 'They're going to take me to the bank and wait outside,' said Russell.

'Perfect,' said Drury. 'It ties in with what I'm going to tell them. Anything else?'

Russell scratched the back of his neck with a fingertip. 'Yeah. The business about the bag is simplified. Jacumb asked me to get one.'

'Perfect,' said Drury again. 'I had a long talk with Judy tonight and she knows the worst. She's with us, Mark.'

Russell pursed his mouth. 'One more one less, what's the difference?'

'I've talked to Emily-May,' said Drury. 'We all know what to do. The important thing to remember is that they're convinced they're going to screw us. That's what's going to do them in, Mark. Now here's the way you play it in the bank . . .'

NINE

Benjy carried his drink to a chair beyond the pool. The string of lamps overhead dotted the deck with light. He pulled his chair into the shadow and sat watching the steps that led down from the Terrace Bar. It was five minutes before his brother appeared, fast-stepping and frog-eyed with excitement. He dropped into the chair beside Benjy, fanning himself with one of the bar menus.

'He went for it,' he said, leaning back and stretching luxuriously. 'He had to wrestle with his conscience but he finally gave it his best. It seems that the Internal Revenue isn't too popular around the Seminary at the moment, but the clincher was envy. I told him if he didn't want to do it a rabbi would.'

'Aiee!' said Benjy. He waited until the clanking and groaning of the chains had subsided. 'Mealy-mouthed hypocrities! I tell you, Shel, these guys are the real con artists. But if you said that on the street you'd have every cop, judge and the mafia jumping all over you.'

'Correct,' said Sheldon who was in good form. 'You should have heard him on the subject of corrupt men in high places. Scoundrels without principle, venal and morally bankrupt. Then there was a bit about private enterprise for the glory of God.'

'What?' said Benjy. '"Private enterprise for the glory of God"? He must have been putting you on.'

'He was drunk,' said Sheldon. 'He promised me tickets for the Notre Dame game. He acted like I was supposed to genuflect or something.'

The *Skagerrak* shuddered as her bows met open water.

The Terrace Bar was closing. No more than half a dozen people were left at the tables.

'You've told him what he has to do?' asked Benjy.

'Sure. He'll have to take his passport and a bag to carry the money. His face'll do the rest. The guy's an out-and-out chump, Benjy.'

'Getting information out of Munro is like trying to take meat from a tiger,' said Benjy. 'I hate the fucker, Shel.'

The boat lifted slightly. They were well out at sea with Haiti no more than a lighter shadow in the darkness behind.

'The banks in San Juan open nine until two-thirty,' said Benjy. 'We dock at eleven. That gives us three and a half hours. It all depends on Munro. He's keeping post time to himself.'

Sheldon yawned. 'Where do you think he'll be?'

'That's easy,' Benjy said with conviction. 'He'll be outside, sitting somewhere around the block with that smirk on his face, waiting for us to bring the money to him. I hate the fucker, Shel!'

'You said.' Sheldon sounded interested. 'Why?'

'He reminds me of the old man.'

'No kidding!' Sheldon sat up straight. 'Now that *is* weird!'

Benjy was talking as much for himself as for Sheldon. 'They've both got this goddamn certainty about everything. Like the old man and his "you kids think you've got the world by the balls". Then he takes that big BUT and rams it up your ass. The truth of it is, *they're* the ones who think that they know it all. I don't care who Munro is or where he comes from, Shel. I want to screw him is all.'

'You want to take five hundred grand away from him.' Sheldon said shrewdly.

Benjy pressed down with his feet, fighting the rise of the deck. 'That too. I fixed everything with Bishirgian. You want to know something, Sheldon? Lansky runs with a very strange crowd down here. This Bishirgian's a hundred and one and lives with an old black mammy and a monkey.

I still stink of the goddamn place.' He sniffed at his clothing and grimaced.

'But you got what you wanted?'

'I got what I wanted.' He pulled the king size cigarette pack from his pocket. 'See this? Inside is the prettiest little peashooter you ever saw. The first sign of trouble from Munro I'm going to stick it in his ear.' He displayed the gun in the palm of his hand.

Some of the lights above had gone out. The angles of Sheldon's face were sharp in the luminosity of the stars.

'I don't know, Benjy. All this boom-boom Bonnie and Clyde stuff worries me.'

Benjy's normally genial expression saddened. 'There are times when you disappoint me, Sheldon.'

Sheldon took the news with equanimity. 'I know it and I don't give a shit.'

'*Trust* me, Sheldon,' urged Benjy. 'Have I ever steered you wrong?'

'Frequently,' said Sheldon. 'The trouble there is that you're my brother. I keep coming back for punishment.'

'Your *big* brother,' Benjy amplified. 'Your *smart* big brother! I'll tell you how Munro intends to play this number. There may be variations but the basic play will be for him not to lose control of the loot. Not for one moment does he intend to let this fat-assed priest walk away with a hundred grand. And he sure isn't going to hand out ten grand apiece to you, me and Nielsen. No, Sheldon. He's going to take a swift hike with the whole caboodle and leave us to pick up the pieces. At least, that's what he *thinks* he's going to do!'

The bar had completely closed. The two brothers were alone on deck. 'What's that you said about the purser on the phone?' asked Sheldon.

'Nothing,' said Benjy. The movement of the boat was not unpleasant and he swayed with it. 'Forget it, I shouldn't have mentioned it.'

'But you did,' Sheldon insisted. 'So tell me.'

'I said it's nothing,' Benjy said expansively. It would

141

never do to describe the incident in the cab. Sheldon was inclined to crank up tight at moments like these. 'Whenever I turn my head the bum seems to be staring at me. That's just me being paranoiac.'

'I don't know,' Sheldon said doubtfully. 'There's too many things could go wrong for my liking. I mean Nielsen for instance. Have you seen him today? He looks like one of his goddamn sheep on speed.'

'I don't wonder,' said Benjy. 'The bum's going to be in big trouble. He'll do what he has to do and then run. Which is all to the good, Shel. While he's running around looking for ways to get off the island, we'll be in Guadaloupe.'

'For how long?'

Benjy's wave was expansive. 'A matter of hours. Lansky's man in San Juan is taking care of everything.'

'Again with the rackets,' said Sheldon. 'And how much is all this costing?'

'Ten grand.' Moisture came on the breeze and Benjy wiped his face. 'What do you want to do, press up against some airline counter and ask to be smuggled through customs? No, Sheldon, you need that sort of protection, you go to the right people.'

Sheldon changed the subject. 'Some bank in Zürich sent Munro ten grand to the bank downstairs. Nielsen told me.'

Benjy smiled appreciation. 'I *thought* that had to be the angle! This is one smart bastard, Sheldon. He's going to crack their code.'

'Nielsen wanted to know did we think we'd get our ten thousand. He didn't say anything about taking off.'

'He leaves the boat tomorrow,' said Benjy. 'And he won't be coming back. And you know something, Sheldon, it'll be the first sensible thing he's done in his whole life.'

Sheldon was staring up at the stars. 'Guadaloupe and then where?'

'Paris,' said Benjy. 'We're there in six hours.'

'Paris.' Sheldon stretched and yawned. 'I've got a couple of phone numbers there.'

His brother's hand found Sheldon's shoulder. 'Tomorrow's going to be our lucky day.'

'Good,' said Sheldon. 'I never did like the idea of a rock pile.'

Benjy's grip tightened. 'There's no way that we're going to be scooped. Trust Benjy. All we have to do is watch our backs and tread daintily.'

His brother's voice broke. Shaldon swallowed. 'I'm not going to let you have it . . .

'Good,' said Shaldon. 'Now we ask the steward to lock up . . .

Emily's lips tightened. I knew this was where it would all be resolved. We would all have to go down with the brass band in red flannel.

TEN

It was already hot and the curtains had been drawn on the starboard side of the restaurant, blocking out the sun. It was just after eight and few of the tables were occupied. The waiters were attentive, eager to get breakfast over. San Juan meant shore leave for most of them. Drury poured himself more coffee, looking across at Judy. The sun had taken a firm hold, splashing her forehead and arms with freckles. She looked about sixteen in her blue checked shirt. She had barely spoken since she had sat down, just staring at him over the top of her coffee cup.

'What is it, baby?' he asked gently.

She moved her head from side to side without answering. It was something she had done since childhood and the refusal to communicate always infuriated him. It was less defiance than obstinacy.

'If you're having a change of heart . . . ' he began.

She reached across and stopped his mouth with her fingers. 'It's not that, Papa. It's just that it's been a long night.'

He nodded, close to what she was talking about. He pictured her lying there in the darkness, surrounded by broken pieces and wondering how she was ever going to put them together again.

A voice sounded over the public address system, dominating the general murmur of conversation.

'Good morning, ladies and gentlemen! This is your purser speaking. We are roughly sixty miles north-north-west of Puerto Rico and making twenty knots an hour. We should arrive in San Juan shortly after eleven hundred hours. Will passengers intending to spend the night ashore kindly notify the bureau in the Main Hall. Thank you!'

Drury pushed away from the table. Russell was across the room alone, eating what appeared to be ham and eggs. The wayward plume of hair rose on the back of his scalp like a war lock and a book was propped open in front of him. Whatever else, Mark would be Mister Cool.

Drury spoke quietly. 'Don't forget, honey, whatever happens you stay real close to Emily-May. OK?' It was the nearest that he would go towards the admittance of failure.

She took her lipstick from her bag. He could see the soft suede roll that contained her jewellery and her passport and wallet inside. She snapped the clasp on the bag.

'Worry about whoever you like, Papa, but not about me. I'm still your daughter and I don't scare that easily.'

He smiled, remembering her as an eight-year-old, blood streaming from a cut eyebrow, demanding to be put back up on the pony that had thrown her. Again, as a twenty-eight-year-old in the study at Orbec, stony faced as she related her nightmare life with her husband. No, cowardice was not part of her nature. She accepted facts and faced them.

He shrugged as she rose. 'Maybe if I had my druthers I wouldn't be here but I am.'

There was half an hour before the bank outside opened. He went back to his cabin and sat down, poring over the cables that Nielsen had given him. The phone rang. It was Russell.

'The moment you left the purser came over to my table. So he sits down, looking over his shoulder all the time and what do you think? He's worried about me. He thinks I'm in the hands of con men.'

'*Sonofabitch!*' said Drury, his mind casting about frantically.

'That's not all,' said Russell. 'He sent a cable to the Dade County Sheriff's Department asking them to check out Jacumb and Black.'

A swooping gull outside was a flash of sunlight on wings. Russell's words seems to hang in the air.

'Don't worry,' said Russell. 'The answer was negative. But the bastard's still sniffing around. Was I sure that I hadn't been propositioned? It seems he's got a nose like a hound for a crook.'

'I'd like to fire a harpoon up his ass,' Drury said bitterly.

'Don't worry,' Russell repeated. 'The good father straightened him out. I told him that Jacumb was a fine young man with a real interest in the church. I thought for a minute he'd choke but he finally swallowed it.'

Drury drew a deep breath. 'I'm going to have a word with Nielsen. The bastard should have told us. Have you seen Emily-May this morning?'

'We spent the night together,' said Russell and hung up.

At five to nine Drury made his way down to the Main Hall. Cleaners were dragging sacks of refuse across the floor, ready for throwing over the side. The radio room was closed. Drury rapped on the shutter. Nielsen opened the door. A battery operated shaver lay on his desk. Drury reached back, locking the door behind him.

'Crissakes,' said Nielsen. 'Somebody might have seen you!'

'Shut up and sit down,' said Drury. Nielsen's breakfast tray was untouched except for the coffee. It was difficult to know whether the smell of liquor on Nielsen's breath came from last night's intake or this morning's.

Drury jerked the drawer open but the bottle of Jim Beam was not there.

'Why didn't you tell me that Voitek had been in touch with the Sheriff's Department?' Drury demanded.

Nielsen's hand was shaking and his eyes were bloodshot. 'I didn't think there was any need. I tore the goddamn cable up and faked the reply. What's to tell?'

'I don't give a shit what you think,' said Drury, pointing

at the lighted panel. 'I told you – I want to know every single word that comes in or goes out of that thing.'

Nielsen shook his head, the shaver buzzing in his hand.

'Don't you understand,' Drury said reasonably. 'We're supposed to be on the same side?'

'Ain't nobody on my side,' Nielsen said bitterly.

'Nobody but me,' said Drury, relenting a little. 'As a breed your associates rank with skunks. But I'm the ray of sunshine at the end of the road. I'm ten bills in an envelope waiting to be sent wherever you want.'

'That's one sawn-off shotgun that just fired a blank!' Nielsen's laugh was hollow. 'You're not giving me no ten grand and you know it!'

'Wrong,' said Drury. It was one minute to nine by the ship's chronometer hanging on the wall. The banks in San Juan were just about to open. 'Ten thousand dollars sent wherever you like.'

Nielsen's eyes shifted furtively. 'I've got a sister in Butte.' He scribbled an address on a piece of paper and laid it on the desk between them. He blew the hairs from his shaver and put it away in its case.

'Those guys are going to screw you. They're pros. Did you ever hear of someone called Lansky?'

Drury shook his head. 'The Mafia man in Miami,' said Nielsen. 'They're friends of his.'

Drury put the address in his pocket. It was a promise that would be kept. He spoke in a quiet reassuring voice.

'Nobody's going to screw me, Ed. Keep that at the front of your head. Now listen. Tefler's going to give you a cable to send in a few minutes. *You do not send it!* What you do is call my room. I'll give you another cable to send in its place. Is that quite clear?'

'As a bell,' said Nielsen. 'I can hear the police sirens from here.'

A light glowed on the panel. Someone wanted to call his daughter in Amarillo. Nielsen made the connection, took off his headphones and looked at Drury. His voice had the shameless whine of the loser.

'I can't take much more of this.'

Drury rose. 'I don't know how good you'll be with sheep but you'd never make a thief. Remember now, the moment Tefler gives that cable, call me!'

He opened the door slightly, choosing his moment to step outside. People were shopping for rolls of film, paperbacks, guide-books. Women besieged the beauty parlour wanting to have their hair fixed before going ashore. The bank was open. Drury walked in. A crewcut youngster was about to cut him off but Tefler came forward.

'Good morning, Mister Munro.'

'I'd like to have a word with you in private,' said Drury.

Tefler opened his office door. 'Come on in.' He turned to the crewcut youngster. 'See that I'm not disturbed, Jim.'

He put himself behind his desk and nodded at the outer office. 'It never fails. They all wait until the last moment to cash in their cheques. They've got this weird idea that they get a better deal aboard ship. Nobody seems to figure that a dollar is a dollar wherever. Now what can I do for you?'

Drury smoothed white hair. 'The money that came in yesterday. I have to send it out again.'

Tefler's professional mask slipped slightly. He was wearing a short-sleeved white-on-white shirt and smelled of some undistinguished cologne.

'OK, you pay the charges, we ship the merchandise.' His pencil hovered above his pad.

'I'd like it to go right now,' said Drury. 'Immediately.'

'No problem,' said Tefler and spoke into the intercom box. 'Bring in Mister Munro's file.'

'A change of plan,' Drury volunteered in the intervening silence.

The girl dropped the folder on Tefler's desk and went out again. 'Now,' said Tefler. 'Where's the money going and to whom?'

Drury gave the address of the Injured Jockeys Fund in London. It was sometimes good to play God. The banker held his pen in his teeth as he searched a drawer for transfer forms. He inked in a couple of crosses.

'If you'll sign where I've marked, Mister Munro. You want the charges to come out of the ten thousand or what?'

'Sure,' said Drury. Some broken-bodied jump jockey lying in traction would still benefit.

'I'll see to this right away,' Tefler promised.

Drury nodded. 'Thanks for your trouble. And don't forget our lunch in Caracas.'

Drury's phone rang a couple of minutes after he reached his cabin. It was Nielsen. 'The girl just brought it in.'

'Close the office,' said Drury. 'I'll be right down.'

A note was affixed to the door of the radio room. *Back in ten minutes.* The door handle turned in Drury's grasp. Nielsen licked his lips like a dog that is unsure of itself.

'This isn't going to work.'

'Sit down!' said Drury, locking the door. 'Now listen to me, buster,' he said venomously. 'I've put a lot into this operation and no chicken-hearted clown is going to ruin it for me.'

Nielsen did his best to hold the stare but failed. His face was haggard under the suntan. Drury composed his own message using Tefler's cable as a guide.

'Get it on the air,' he said, looking up and passing the cable across the desk.

Nielsen flexed his fingers like a concert pianist, sweat springing on his forehead. The typewriter clattered. Drury pulled the form from the rollers.

21 Code/Clear
Kastrupbank
San Juan Puerto Rico
M.V. *Skagerrak*
Rpt

Balsa/Carat Credit Father Jerzy Mitrega holder
U.S. Passport 2637589 five hundred thousand

dollars, U.S. 500 000 stop Walkaway present-
ation stop Kastrupbank M.V. *Skagerrak*
21 Code Clear
Kastrupbank
San Juan Puerto Rico
M.V. *Skagerrak*
Rpt

'Send it!' said Drury.

Nielsen put on the headphones, hand shaking as he held the microphone. Drury could just hear a voice at the other end, repeating the message.

'Right,' said Drury. 'Now send the cable to London.'

He took his hand from the other man's shoulder. 'When they check back the cables come to me. I'll tell you what to do.'

Nielsen tried to light a cigarette but failed with three matches. His control had completely gone. Drury helped him.

'Look,' said Drury. 'Pull yourself together. You're almost out of the wood.'

His bed had been made and there were clean towels in the bathroom. It was too early for a cigar but he lit one nevertheless. The tailors' labels had been removed from his clothes. There was nothing left that would identify him. He opened a porthole and sat down facing it, the sea breeze blowing in his face. He hadn't felt better in years. There was a special pleasure in dispensing rough justice to rogues who richly deserved it. His thoughts drifted to Judy. The shadow between them would lift and they'd be even closer than before. Maybe she would find the right guy and give him the grandson he had always wanted.

He jumped and reached for the ringing telephone. Nielsen's voice was drained of expression.

'I've got the bank in San Juan on the line, wanting to talk to Tefler!'

Drury's brain raced into action. 'Put 'em on to me! And

for crissakes get a hold on yourself!' The line clicked into the connection.

'Tefler speaking,' said Drury.

The voice was unmistakeably British. 'Fowler, San Juan. We just received your cable.'

'Yes,' Drury said guardedly.

'The code's wrong,' said Fowler. 'The letters don't match the amount. I'll read you what we have here. Balsa/Credit which is obviously wrong if the amount is right. Five hundred thousand?'

'Check,' said Drury. 'Five hundred thousand United States dollars. There must have been a fault in transmission.' Sweat was rolling down his flanks from his armpits. He walked the knife edge, waiting for the other man's reply.

'That's rather what we thought,' answered Fowler. 'OK, I'll read it back as amended.'

Drury listened. 'I'll have a word with the radio room,' he said when the other man had finished.

'Right,' said Fowler. 'But obviously we had to check. Who's your priest, has he won the Irish Sweep or something?'

Drury opened his eyes again, salt from the sweat had run into them. 'I don't think so, no. The funds came from Rome.'

Fowler laughed. 'That's where it's all happening. When are we going to meet? What are you doing for lunch?'

'I'm tied up,' said Drury. 'Maybe next trip. Thanks for letting me know about the cable. I'll go next door and give them hell!'

'Do that,' said Fowler. 'It's been nice talking to you and put your amended text in the mail for the records.'

'The moment we dock,' promised Drury. 'Goodbye!'

He put the phone down and redialled. 'Try to keep your knees from knocking,' he said to Nielsen. 'Everything's been taken care of.'

Nielsen hiccoughed. 'We're off the air for the next hour

and a half. Instructions from the United States Navy.
We're in their waters now.'

'Good,' said Drury. 'It'll give you time to sober up before
you go ashore.'

ELEVEN

It was sixteen minutes past eleven. The *Skagerrak* was nosing into the Bay of San Juan. The passengers had crowded to the starboard side of the ship, armed with cameras and binoculars. The green spine of the island showed in the distance, the lakes and teak forests below. Everyone moved to the port side as the ship passed under the beetling sandstone walls of the fort. A Miami Beach like shoreline spiked the sky beyond Old San Juan.

Nielsen watched it all with growing apprehension. This was no banana republic. San Juan was a sophisticated city of half a million, policed by stateside trained cops, drug enforcement agencies, the F.B.I. and the whole fandangled business. He feared the very worst for the assault on the Hastrupbank and secretly he was glad. He would happily forego his ten grand if only these three smart-assed bastards would get their comeuppance. But for the moment he wanted out just as fast as he could travel.

He was standing at one of the radio room windows, watching the shoreline glide by. Across the Bay tourists were sunning themselves on the crescent-shaped beaches, preparing for a nightlife that finished with dawn. It was a scene that had never tempted him. When other kids had been thinking of getting it on with one another's sisters he'd been dreaming of sheep and a horse. Later on, maybe, there'd be a permanent live-in girlfriend who wouldn't try to trap him with kids. The dream had been nurtured ever since he was fifteen years old and he had staked high to make it come true. His downfall had started with his meeting a stripper called Clara Sacucci who had intro-

duced him to Lansky who had sent the Californians. The
rollercoaster ride had been a fast one from there.

Bells were ringing all over the ship as they docked.
Engines were reversed, swinging the *Skagerrak* parallel
with the pier. Passengers and crew would disembark to
pass through no more than a token inspection by customs
and immigration officers. The radio room was still locked.
The naval ban on communications had been genuine.
Nielsen had simply extended it. The notice pinned to the
outside of the door now read that no business could be
accepted until 1530 hours. Crew members were entitled to
take shore leave in civilian clothing. Nielsen had changed
his mind and had on a blue cotton shirt, J.C. Penney jeans
and sneakers. He looked the way he always wanted to
look, insignificant. Everything except what was in his
pockets had been left in his cabin. Head office had his
history since grade school but they would have a tough
time tracing him. His only living relative was his sister and
they didn't have her address. If anyone wanted to search
him on landing they'd find his bank book, union card and
passport and what little money he'd been able to take from
the Californians. Sons of bitches!

A series of bumps told him that the *Skagerrak* was being
berthed. Ropes snaked ashore to the accompaniment of
excited yelling in Spanish. Nielsen could see the cops on
the pier, standing in the shade, big spic bastards with jazzy
caps and dark glasses. Dock workers ran the wheeled
gangways forward and seamen made them fast. Nielsen
watched the first passengers disembark. The two Californians and the fat little priest were among them. It was
some time before the big white haired guy appeared, the
two women close behind as they walked down the
gangway. Railings at the end of the pier sealed off the Calle
Marina. Beyond the railings was a blur of faces. Cab drivers
leaned on their horn buttons vying for custom.

It was hot, noisy and colourful out there and a long way
from Montana. Nielsen emptied the last of the Thermos
flask into a paper cup. He had been drinking iced rum and

coconut milk for the last two hours. There was no way now that he could stop. He had to keep going with it. The stream of disembarking passengers dwindled and then finally dried up. Nielsen opened the door. The Main Hall was deserted and strangely silent. Everything was closed, bank, bureau and shops. Only a skeletal crew was left aboard in San Juan. The rest were going down the gangways in twos and threes, heading for the bars of Old San Juan.

Nielsen crossed the Hall. Someone was still inside the bank. He could hear a machine of some kind working. That would be Tefler. The bank manager trusted neither foreign food, water nor money and was known never to put a foot ashore from the beginning of a cruise to the end. Nielsen was just about to step onto the gangway when he heard his name called from behind. He turned sharply. The purser was leaning against a ventilator, still dressed in his uniform whites.

'Hi!' he said, coming off the ventilator and sauntering forward. His eyes took in the details of Nielsen's appearance. 'What's this notice on the door? What happens in an emergency?'

'You swim ashore and yell for help,' Nielsen answered. It was typical of this weasel-faced mother to find a question like that.

Voitek showed no intention of letting Nielsen go. 'Where did the authority come from?'

'It came from the United States Navy,' said Nielsen, 'and the bridge has a copy of the signal. Why don't you take it up with them if you're feeling argumentative?'

Pleasure boats were skimming the water. A plane jetted out overhead. Precious moments were ticking away and this clown wanted to make conversation.

Voitek's face was curious. 'Whatsamatter, Nielsen, you been drinking again? You've been acting very strange this cruise.'

'Overwork is what's the matter,' Nielsen replied. 'Working sixteen hours a day and sending bullshit messages to places like the Dade County Sheriff's Department.'

'That's what I wanted to see you about,' said Voitek. 'I've been through those bastards' cabins with a fine tooth comb and I didn't find a thing.'

'What did you expect to find?' It would be easy for Voitek to get hold of a passkey.

The purser smiled narrowly. 'I've got an idea that Dade County fouled-out. I intend to contact the F.B.I. about Mister Black and Mister Jacumb and I don't mean the field office here. I'm talking about Washington. What time will you be back on board?'

Nielsen thought quickly. The last thing he wanted was Voitek ashore making trouble.

'I'll be back around five. I can raise Washington for you right away.'

Voitek's dark face closed with secret thoughts. 'There are a couple of ideas that I want to run down. I'll see you at five and, Ed . . .'

'What's on your mind?'

Voitek tilted an invisible glass. 'I'd watch it if I were you. The old man will be on the bridge when you get back.'

Nielsen walked through both checks unmolested and hailed the first cab that he saw. He leaned back hard on the seat.

'Isla Verde!'

The driver grinned. 'Jou going and jou joost got in? Whassamarer, jou don like us?'

'Love you,' said Nielsen and shut his eyes. The driver was a city boy who drove nervously, his long brown thumb never far from the horn button.

They drove across town, picking up the freeway to the International Airport. Nielsen added a dollar to the fare and exchanged the glare and heat for the refrigerated coolness of the terminal building. The interior was full of women with screaming children, the noise and indiscipline of a Caribbean airport. The times and destinations of departing planes were displayed on a board. The first flight out was to Mexico City, the second to Toronto. This left in fifty-five minutes time. He went to the Eastern Airlines counter, prepared to bluff or bribe his way onto the flight but there was space enough to offer choice of an aisle or window seat.

The girl took his cash, wrote up the ticket and gave him his boarding card.

'Gate C in half an hour's time, sir, and have a good flight!'

He put on a pair of dark glasses and bought a newspaper to hide his face with. It was almost noon and he'd be in Toronto just after five. There was no question now of going to Montana. He'd have to bus back over the border and head south. He lolled against the Nalgahyde couch and narrowed his eyes behind the dark glasses. He'd been making wrong decisions for years, only this time the choice had been made for him. And maybe it wasn't too bad at that.

The smart thing to do was empty his bank account, get the hell out of the U.S. of A. and stay out. He smiled without knowing it, a feeling of freedom and movement suddenly making him tolerant of the scene around. Men and women in cheap finery were clutching string-tied packages. Good old United States citizens on their way north to freeze their balls off in New York. They'd live in South Bronx and the kids would learn to shoot smack and mug old ladies. They ought to stay down here in the sun. Everything was better in the sun including a bald head.

The edge had gone from the booze he had drunk on the boat. He heaved himself up and walked across to the bar. The black landing strips outside were wilting in the intense heat. The windows of the airplanes parked there flashed reflected sunshine. He ordered a triple Bacardi with a tonic mix and carried the drink back to the bench. No sir, he was going to play it real cool from now on. There'd be no more screwing around with racket guys and the hell with the sheep. He sank two inches of his drink and crushed a lump of ice between his back teeth.

The display flickered on the departure board and his eyes focussed on *Mexico City*. Why not, he thought suddenly. There'd be no problem down there for a good radio man. In fact, a couple of years work and you could buy a piece of land down there in Baja California, grow some good grass and dig for *abalones*. A vision of a girl grew in his mind, lithe and black eyed with tilted brown breasts and ropes of shiny hair. She'd be cooking up that good Mex food while he drifted in a dinghy, smoking dope, as high as an elephant's eye.

He was forty-two years old and it was finally coming together. Shit, he could swing a deal like that right now if he wanted to! He had the best part of twenty grand in the Deer Lake Federal Savings. He had seen how easily these things could be arranged. All he'd have to do would be walk into some bank in Mexico City, sign a piece of paper and presto!

The departure board blinked again, the tiny shutters reforming the times and destinations. He walked across to the bar and ordered the same. The Puerto Rican splashed tonic into a tall frosted glass and added a triple shot of rum. Nielsen frowned as the ice cubes dropped in.

'Wrong way round, buddy!'

The barman grinned nervously as though Nielsen had said something risqué.

'Wrong way round,' Nielsen repeated. He didn't pick fights with barmen but these things mattered.

'*Pardon, señor!*' The barman retained his smile and his dignity. Nielsen nodded to show that he was a regular guy. It was just that certain things had to be done right. He walked back to his seat, treading on large balloons. Mexico, all that space! They said you could live for free down there in Baja. So what was this with Toronto? All that ice and snow and a wind coming off the lake that would cut your balls off. You'd pay your rent in advance and there'd be no-one but the law to care whether you lived or died. He needed his head examined.

He stared across the hall to the Mexican Airlines counter. An impulse took him and he lifted his arm and waved. The girl at the counter turned her head quickly. Better watch it, he thought. This stuff's beginning to get to me. No, what you needed to ride out this sort of situation was class and he had class in plenty. Hell, a dime call to the Kastrupbank and every single one of these motherfuckers would be on the rock pile. But he was no fink and there was the question of self-preservation. Class or no class, you had to protect yourself. If he blew the whistle now, the law would be jumping all over the island.

He lurched a little as he came upright and moved towards the Mexican Airlines counter. He laid his Eastern Airlines ticket in front of the girl.

'Hi, beautiful! I'd like to trade this in for a ticket to Mayheeko City.'

To his own ears he sounded persuasive. The old charm was still there.

The girl was good looking and well mannered. 'I am sorry, *señor*, but we cannot exchange this ticket. You must have it cancelled by Eastern Airlines.'

By craning a little he could see her size 36B cups and the mole that grew between her breasts.

'Fair enough,' he said largely, waiving the point. 'I'd just like to be on the next flight, sweetheart. I guess you can handle that for me, can't you?'

She pressed a button and consulted the computer screen in front of her.

'Yes, *señor*, that would be possible.' She hesitated. 'I am sorry, *señor*, but it is not allowed to drink at the counter.'

He glanced down at the glass in his hand, surprised to see it there. He emptied it at a draft and left the glass where it was on the counter.

'I'll be right back,' he promised and moved down the

concourse to the Eastern Airlines office. They cancelled his ticket and he took his voucher to the cashier. They were quick enough to take your money but not so damn quick about giving it back.

He had less than fifteen minutes before the flight was scheduled to leave. The girl had his new ticket ready but needed his name and nationality.

'Edward Nielsen, American.' His empty glass had disappeared. He gave her the money, staring hard at her breasts.

'Habla Español, señorita?' he asked on impulse.

She looked up, surprised. 'Pero si, señor. Jo soy Mexicana!'

He leaned across, whispering. 'Then how about you and me next time you're in Mayheeko City, know what I mean?' He showed her his thumb between his fingers.

Her face froze and then flamed. She dropped the pad she was holding and swung hard with the flat of her right hand. She was small but all the weight of her body was behind the blow. Its force jerked Nielsen's head sideways. Tears welled in the girl's eyes but she held her ground. A half-circle of curious faces assembled. Nielsen took his fingers from his mouth and looked at them. No blood. Sonofabitch! He grinned weakly and took a few steps in the direction of the Exit Gates.

A hand touched his shoulder from behind. The cop was both large and Latin but the language was familiar. 'What seems to be the problem, buddy?'

The guy was an echo of every cop that Nielsen had seen, read or dreamed about. Shark-toothed and shark-eyed and wearing some sort of outrageous gun in a tooled leather holster. Nielsen's mind grew paranoiac. After twenty-five dreary assed years dot-dashing geek radio operators for a crummy living he was on his way to heaven when suddenly trouble was coming at him from every direction.

A great calm spread over Nielsen because the voice was about to speak. It wasn't his own voice but that of

Eduardo, the much-loved beachcomber who spoke for him in a sort of simian snarl.

'The problem, buddy? The problem is that there are too many shitheads like you around.'

The cop smiled with enjoyment and leaned forward. 'I didn't quite get that.'

'What are you, hard of hearing?' Eduardo demanded. 'Now get off my back before I turn my Black Belt loose on you.'

Those standing nearest the couple moved away hurriedly as the cop's large hands reached out. Nielsen's arms were jerked behind his back and the lift took him into space. The handcuffs snapped shut just as his eyes sought the clock. The plane for Mexico City took off in exactly four minutes.

TWELVE

Drury had never been in Puerto Rico let alone in San Juan. Everything was strange. The front of the Maritime Building was a vortex of movement and noise. He walked slowly past porters and cab drivers lounging in the shade, street vendors hawking coconut milk and *pasteles*. He crossed the street and turned left on Calle Tetuan. He was now on the border of Old San Juan, a seven-block city guarded by sixteenth century forts and a sandstone wall forty feet high. What was enclosed within the wall remained as it had been built. Colonial houses with balconies overlooked narrow streets. There were glimpses of wide stairways, teak beams and flower-bedecked patios. Craftsmen working with leather and metal sat in dark rooms lit by single hanging lamps.

Sunshine sharply divided the streets, creeping past one whitewashed surface through wrought iron lattices on to the wall opposite. Timeless and spiced with history, the old city's commerce depended on its bars and restaurants, its boutiques and arts and crafts shops selling fringed straw hats, rag dolls and bamboo birdcages. Humble *tiendas* infested with flies sold fish and dried meat by the fifty grammes and the dogs were lean and hungry. Poverty thrust out its hand from the shadows, silently pleading for alms.

The address Drury wanted was on a corner of Calle O'Donnell. It was a four storey sandstone building in the Hispanic tradition. A sign, illuminated at night, hung above the imposing entrance steps: Kastrupbank (Incorporated in the Kingdom of Denmark) Branches throughout the Caribbean. Drury's guide-book devoted half a page to the edifice. Erected in 1890, it had been designed by Aino Dudek, architect and Hispanophile. The building had taken two years and eight months to complete and featured two roofed arcaded galleries overlooking a central banking hall.

Drury took his bearings. The angle at which the bank entrance was set allowed anyone high in the vast parking building two blocks away to observe people coming and going. Drury eased his belt a notch and took the shady side of the street to the Carol Cruz Foto Supply Store. He bought a pair of lightweight twelve-power glasses and continued along the street as far as a stand-up coffee bar. He walked straight through into the lavatory and locked himself in a fouled cubicle. He broke the covers of his false passport and burned each page separately. Acrid smoke filled the cubicle. He flushed the ashes away, washed his hands in rusty water and went out again. Mark's false book was needed for the bank. Drury's progress now was a gentle saunter up the rise to Calle Fortaleza. He waited as a man handrolled ten cigars from island grown tobacco. His next stop was El Corte Elegante. In a country where large waists and fat behinds are common, Russell's requirements were easy to fit. Drury bought a pair of cotton trousers and a flowered panelled shirt with four outside pockets. A block west, Apex Rental supplied a blue Dodge and honoured Drury's international driving licence. He threaded the Dodge through the complicated one-way system back to the parking building. A dollar bill ensured him space at street level. He left the car unlocked and in plain view of the pedestrians' entrance. It was just after noon as he walked north along cobblestoned alleyways to a bar at the foot of one of the step-streets. The Bodega Malaga was reached down a flight of stone stairs. At the bottom was a cool dim room smelling of garlic soup. The wall behind the bar was covered with old bullfight posters. Trays on top of sherry casks offered a selection of *tapas*. Prawns in hot sauce, fried squid, olives stuffed with anchovies.

He bought a glass of fino from a sleepy-eyed woman and took it out to a flagged patio. A stone dolphin jetted water into a basin filled with drowned bugs. Emily-May and Judy were sitting under a hibiscus tree. Except for themselves, the place was empty. He pulled a chair and sat down beside them. Judy had found a copy of the local English language daily and was doing the crossword puzzle.

'Hi!' said Emily-May. She was sitting up very straight, a large shopping basket at her side. 'Did you watch the little man leave the ship? So brave – like Sydney Carton.'

Drury thought about it for a moment. 'Definitely not like Sydney Carton,' he decided. 'But very brave.'

Sunshine streaming through the ironwork threw a pattern across Judy's face. She pushed a strand of hair from in front of her eyes.

'You look like a cat with a butter-pat. Do you know something, I can't remember a single thing that you weren't always sure about.'

He grinned. A new dimension seemed to have been added to their relationship.

'This time I'm not only sure, I'm certain.' It was an act of faith. The alternative was unthinkable. 'You both saw the parking building?'

Emily-May nodded. 'The big place opposite the cinema?'

'The car's just inside the entrance on the first floor. A blue Dodge. It's unlocked.' He gave them the licence plate numbers.

Emily-May's outsize shopping basket appeared to be stuffed with articles bought in the arts and crafts stores.

'When do you want us in the bank?' she asked. Her voice was slightly tense.

'In a few minutes,' he said easily. 'You don't want to get there too early and be noticed. Everything has to look natural, a chance meeting.'

Emily-May sniffed. 'You're looking at me in a very peculiar manner, Phil Drury. I may not be as cool as Judy but a degree of anxiety is admissible in the circumstances. I'm an old lady.'

It was Judy who laughed. 'We're all scared to death. The trick is not to show it. Right, Papa?'

'Right,' he agreed. 'The thing is that whatever happens you head straight back for the car. OK?'

He kissed each woman in turn. The Virginian Wonder, his daughter, a dizzy old broad and a fat little con man. 'You're beautiful,' he said, 'and I'm proud of you.'

'You'd better be,' said Judy. 'We don't do this sort of thing too often.' She gathered her bag and her newspaper.

He accompanied them to the bottom of the stone stairs, allowed them fifteen minutes and walked back to the parking building. There were few cars up on the tenth floor. He propped himself on the rear end of a Cadillac and trained his binoculars through the latticed concrete. It was ten minutes past one when a Chrysler sedan drew up in front of the bank. Russell emerged carrying a bag. He waddled up the bank steps and disappeared through the entrance. Seconds later, Jacumb and Black climbed out and followed.

THIRTEEN

The cab driver turned his vehicle off the Expressway onto an escape road. The grade was steep, descending one in four before levelling out again. Giant cacti grew on each side of the road, their spiked fleshy leaves glistening with spiders' webs. Loose dirt that had blown onto the hardtop made the tyres sing. They were somewhere between San Juan Central Park and the Puento Nuevo River but they might well have been in the middle of a desert so still was everything.

It was just noon and the heat was fierce. Palms and candle-trees showed up ahead, linked by strands of barbed wire. An iron gate blocked the way. The driver trod on the brakes and pointed at a sign: *Perro Feroz*. Benjy shrugged. The driver bent his head and seized his own wrist in his teeth, growling like a dog.

'I have no stomach for this,' he said in Spanish. 'Four dollars, sixty cents.'

Benjy gave him a five dollar bill. 'What did he say?' Sheldon asked anxiously.

'Something about a dog,' Benjy answered. They both climbed out. The cab reversed and drove off at speed.

'You know I don't like dogs,' Sheldon complained as the dust subsided.

'So you'll be brave,' said Benjy.

Sheldon shook his head. Sweat streaked the dust on his face and neck. 'If ever I do get out of this I'm going to spend six months straight, on my back telling the shrink about this sadistic brother I've got.'

166

'When you pay the bill, remember where the money comes from,' Benjy answered.

The sound of the cab dwindled in the distance. Benjy lifted the latch on the gate. The name J.E. Spinoza was painted on a locked mail box.

A luxurious carpet of ferns spread beneath the trees on both sides of the driveway. The thought of what might be crawling in there made Benjy's skin creep. Native Californians, neither man was accustomed to walking. He glanced down at his thin soled shoes.

'It's half a mile if a yard,' he said, nodding towards the white house in the distance.

Sheldon shrugged wearily, wiping the dirt from his neck. 'This is going to be another Mustachio Pete with the boom-boom and the drama. I can sense it from here.'

'Let's get it over,' said Benjy.

The sound of dogs barking grew louder as they approached the long low house. It was built in Spanish style with a red tile roof and a verandah running along the entire front. Jacaranda and hibiscus splashed the walls with colour. Bamboo birdcages hung from the ceiling of the verandah. An Olympic-size pool to the right of the house was fringed with coconut palms and thatched cabanas.

The dogs stopped barking as Benjy and Sheldon stepped onto the verandah. Sheldon's face paled.

'Goddamn, Benjy,' he said in a loud whisper.

There was no sign of life from the house, just the distant sound of a lawn-mower and the twittering of the caged finches. Through the large picture windows they could see an elaborately furnished room with silk rugs spread over a tiled floor. A piece of sheet music was propped open in front of a small grand piano. The chairs and tables were red, gold and black. Giant Chinese vases flanked the empty fireplace. Sheldon touched the strips of hanging glass.

'It's open.'

There was dogshit on Benjy's shoe and he scraped it off on the side of the verandah.

'Anyone home?' he yelled. This was Haiti all over again.

A swarthy hand parted the glass screen. Its owner was short and in his late sixties. He was wearing a flowered shirt outside his trousers, a bandit's moustache and a heavy gold crucifix around his neck. He had a thatch of steel grey hair and a look of undershot belligerence. He gave each of the brothers a bone-crushing handshake.

'The driver found you all right?' He spoke with a strong Brooklyn accent.

'He wouldn't bring us to the house,' said Benjy. 'He didn't seem to like your dog.'

'Dogs,' corrected Spinoza. 'We had a little trouble here, back end of last year. Some gonif prowling around outside. The dogs just about took his arm off. Which of you's Benjy?'

Benjy tapped himself on the chest. 'This is my brother Sheldon. He's not too fond of dogs either.'

'Whatsamatter you don't like dogs?' Sheldon's tightly tailored trousers and yellow top did not appear to find favour with their host.

'I got bitten as a kid.'

The explanation only deepened Spinoza's disapproval. 'Step inside,' he said grudgingly.

The room was even larger than it had looked from outside. Like the verandah it ran the entire width of the house. A woman's bag lay on the piano stool. A cigarette was burning in an ashtray. Spinoza opened a cupboard.

He mixed white rum with fresh pineapple juice and coconut cream in a blender and served the drinks in tall glasses.

Benjy wet his lips politely. 'So why did you want to see us?'

Before Spinoza could answer three Dobermans burst through the doorway and skidded to a halt on the tiles. They stood there quivering, lips retracted over their teeth, staring at Benjy and Sheldon. A low uncertain rumble came from the throat of the largest. Spinoza snapped his fingers and all three dogs sank on their rumps.

'You're safe because you're in the room with me,' he said. 'You wouldn't stand a chance alone. The things that go on in this neighbourhood are terrible. Kids with knives, muggings, rape. All that kind of shit. The dogs are out all night.'

One of the dogs investigated Sheldon's legs then lifted its sleek head with an unwinking stare. Sheldon swallowed hard. Spinoza grinned and snapped his fingers again. The dogs moved to the window, their attention drawn by something outside.

'Lansky said . . . ' started Benjy.

Spinoza cut him short, jabbing his finger from an arrogant posture. 'Screw Lansky! Lansky carries about as much clout down here as the Girl Guides. Your plane's already out at the field. The pilot could fly you up an elephant's ass. He took a crop sprayer straight through Castro's artillery to get himself out of Cuba.'

Sheldon was still looking apprehensive. 'That's great,' said Benjy.

Spinoza took up a position in front of the empty fireplace. 'I talked with Lansky last night after you called. I like to know who I'm dealing with.'

'That's nice,' Benjy said courteously. 'And how was Lansky?'

'How the hell should I know? We talked, we didn't hold hands. Anyway, Lansky don't guarantee your money.'

Benjy blinked and then put his glass down. 'You got to be kidding! Since when does Lansky have to guarantee anything for us?'

Spinoza ran through the question, displaying a couple of thousand dollars worth of dentistry.

'He says you're a couple of regular guys but he don't guarantee your money.'

Sheldon's voice was dangerously quiet. 'What's the matter, you don't hear so good? Benjy just told you. We don't *need* Lansky's guarantee.'

Benjy cleared his throat. Heat, the walk and the dogs had combined to make Sheldon edgy. In a mood like this he could be relied upon to put his foot squarely in anyone's mouth.

'There's no problem with the money,' Benjy said hastily.

Spinoza's undershot jaw retracted a little. 'If there's no problem with money, there's no problem.'

Sheldon came out of his listening attitude. 'Does your pilot drink, uncle? I've got this thing about drinking and driving.'

A vein wormed in Spinoza's neck. He seemed to be having difficulty in breathing. 'What was that again?'

'I asked does the pilot drink?'

'The name!' Spinoza said furiously. 'The name you just called me!'

Sheldon's thin face was innocent. 'You mean "uncle"? You don't like it?'

Spinoza's eyes burned like lasers. 'Of *course* he fucking well drinks! But he don't drink when he's driving! Whatsamatter with this clown?' he demanded of Benjy.

'He doesn't mean anything,' Benjy said hurriedly.

Spinoza's fury pitched on Sheldon again. He seemed unable to let it go.

'Respect!' he said darkly, pointing his finger again.

'Yeah, yeah, I'm sorry!' Sheldon ran it off quickly.

The crucifix swung as Spinoza nodded heavily. 'Half the trouble in the world today, no respect. You two are cleared for a trip around the outer islands. You'll be in Guadaloupe by five o'clock. I'll be at the airport to wave goodbye and collect the ten grand.'

'Fine,' said Benjy, still polite. 'Is it all right for us to go now? We have work to do.'

Spinoza snapped a triple leash on the dogs, holding them back as they strained towards the front door. He shouted something in Spanish and a white jeep drew up in front of the verandah. A negro youth smoking a cigar was at the wheel.

'He'll take you to your car,' said Spinoza, still restraining the dogs. 'I'll be waiting in front of the Terminal Building. I'll be there at three.'

Benjy and Sheldon climbed into the back of the jeep. 'A real sweet guy,' said Sheldon as the driver meshed gears. 'Gets off on his dogs savaging people.'

They bounced high as the driver put his foot down. He took the jeep past the pool and the tennis court onto a back road that meandered through pineapple patches growing on the edge of a mangrove swamp. They climbed a cutoff onto the Kennedy Highway and drove north. Benjy eased his buttocks. It was the first time he had been in a jeep and he thought little of the suspension.

'You were real cute back there,' he said. '"Uncle"! Half a million dollars sitting there waiting for us and he has to be cute!'

'Fuck him,' said Sheldon. 'Who does he think he is, Al Capone?'

'I'll tell you who he is,' Benjy said heavily. 'He's our friend.'

Sheldon half closed his eyes against the wind. 'Sure, for ten grand he's our friend. Without that, all the respect in the world wouldn't get that plane off the ground.'

Benjy glanced sideways. 'Know something, Sheldon? You've got a very nasty attitude towards people at times.'

'That's right,' Sheldon said indifferently. 'People are assholes.'

Benjy looked over the driver's shoulder. They were clocking close to eighty miles an hour and the motor was whining dangerously.

'Slow down!' Benjy yelled.

The driver glanced up in the rearview mirror and shifted his cigar. '*Coche muy fuerte, no?*'

'The guy's a dingbat!' said Benjy. As if to prove it, the driver swung left and left again in a U-turn. Then he swerved and took the exit on squealing rubber, dropped down past a grove of eucalyptus trees and braked in front

171

of a roadside café. It was a squat building with a tin chimney and a large Pepsi-Cola sign. Hens were scrabbling in the dirt out front. People were eating and drinking on rough benches and tables under a primitive canopy. A banner flapping over the eating area read: *Cold Beer Jumbo Prawns All You Can Eat and Drink for $4.00.*

A dark green Chrysler sedan was parked under an enormous jacaranda tree. Spinoza's driver passed back a set of ignition keys and nodded at the Chrysler.

'*Adios, señores!*'

He was out of sight, trailing dust, before they reached the parked car. The tyres were new and the needle on the petrol gauge was set at full. A large map of San Juan with a key to the principal places lay open across the steering wheel. Benjy took the driver's seat. A barefooted man peered out from the doorway as Benjy started the engine. They drove back to the city by way of Miramar and stopped near the waterfront bus terminal. Benjy pulled across to the end of Pier One. They were no more than a couple of hundred yards from the *Skagerrak.* The excitement engendered by the cruise ship's arrival had passed and the pier was empty.

A bug had bitten Sheldon. He touched the swelling on the back of his neck with delicate feeling. 'You want to bet Nielsen isn't still up there sucking on a bottle of Jim Beam?'

Benjy shook his head. 'He's long gone. Nielsen isn't the type to sit around and wait for the big bang.'

He pulled the king-size cigarette pack from his pocket and took a look at the tiny gun.

Sheldon's face was disapproving. 'You show that thing to the priest and he'll freak. Don't forget his bad heart.'

'His heart'll be a whole lot worse by the time we're through with him,' said Benjy.

His latest idea was to take the priest with them to the airport and keep him there until the plane took off. If Spinoza's hoods didn't drop him in a sewer he could always start walking.

172

'What about Munro?' asked Sheldon.

Benjy weighed the small weapon in his palm. Its feel was reassuring. 'This takes care of Munro.'

Sheldon was still playing around with the bite on his neck. 'We still don't know where he's going to be.'

'He's going to be sitting outside the bank,' Benjy said confidently. 'Directing traffic. It's a beautiful idea if you think about it. The one guy who can't take a fall is Munro. But he's got a surprise coming to him.' He put the gun back in his pocket.

'Are you going to take him to the airport?'

Benjy stared through the open window. 'Ah yes, Shel, I am! I wouldn't miss that for the world.'

'So laugh,' said Sheldon, looking at his fingers and grimacing. 'But I've got a very peculiar feeling about all this. It's all coming too easily.'

'You frown too much and it doesn't suit you.' Benjy looked at his watch. 'Let's get it on.'

They walked west on the Paseo de la Princessa. Father Mitrega had found shade near the old disused jail. His panama hat was tilted over his eyes and a book lay open in his lap.

'Look at him,' Sheldon said reprovingly. 'Just about to cop a hundred grand in crooked money and he's talking to Jesus!'

The top of the priest's zip was open and he was breathing heavily. He jumped, hearing Sheldon's greeting. 'Hi there, Father!'

The priest's neck was flecked with blood where he had cut himself shaving. He glanced at his watch and shook his head. The book on his knees was the life of Saint Ignatius Loyola.

'I must have dropped off,' he said. 'I was in the church of San Jose.'

'That's nice,' said Sheldon. The priest's bag was on the bench beside him. Sheldon snapped the locks open. The bag was empty. 'All set for the pay off, Father?' Sheldon grinned and winked.

The priest did his zip up. 'I wish you wouldn't use those terms,' he said gently. 'It makes me feel like a criminal.'

Benjy drifted over. 'Father Mitrega's right. We're helping the church and we're helping my family. You might even get promotion, Father!' He crowned a modest cough with a smile.

'I'm afraid not,' said the priest. 'The doctors advised a sea voyage after my coronary. The bishop has been very good to me. It'll be fine to be able to do something in return.'

'Where'd you get the bag?' Sheldon asked curiously. It was plainly new.

'From the shop on the *Skagerrak*. $13.95. You said I'd need something strong.'

'I guess we'd better go,' said Sheldon. Father Mitrega hauled himself up.

'I don't think you understand the kind of pressures we're under,' Benjy said expansively. 'I've given away the best part of a million dollars to charity over the past four years. I figured it was about time that my family benefited.'

'I suppose so,' said the priest. His qualms appeared to have vanished. 'We all live under pressure of one kind or another. More's the pity. There's a lot to be said for the contemplative life.'

'Absolutely,' said Sheldon and opened the rear door of the Chrysler. They put Mitrega in the back seat. Sheldon swung around. 'I'm holding you to that promise, Father. Two tickets for the Notre Dame game.'

'I wish there was more that I could do in return for your generosity,' said the priest. 'But you can rest assured that you'll both be in my prayers.'

'That's really neat,' said Sheldon. Benjy pulled around the block and stopped opposite the bank entrance. 'We'll wait here, Father. It shouldn't take you long.'

They watched the short fat figure carrying the bag climb the steps. Sheldon lit a cigarette, frowning over the match flame.

'It's gone noon. Where the fuck is Munro?'

Benjy glanced up and down the street. 'He'll be here. Let's go!'

The banking hall was designed on the open plan with solid teak rails sealing off the vice-presidential areas. Everything was ordered to relieve stress. Piped music, comfortable benches and chairs, desks plentifully stocked with writing materials. Television screens showed prices at the world's principal stock markets. A couple of hundred voluble and colourful people were enclosed within a space half the size of a football field. The two men turned left and climbed the stairs to the mezzanine floor where they took up position opposite the gilded cages of the tellers. At the back of the cages was a vast mural commemorating Ponce de Leon and the Taino Indians.

Benjy craned forward. 'There he is!' Father Mitrega was at a desk in one of the vice-presidential enclosures, talking to a grizzled man in a seersucker suit. His hat was off and his head was shiny with sweat. Benjy was breathing more quickly than usual. There was no sign of Munro. The bank official had the priest's passport open in front of him and was checking it against some papers. Their dialogue continued for a few minutes then both of them rose. The man in the seersucker suit stood aside to give the priest precedence and they stopped in front of an unmanned teller's cage. A woman in black appeared and the bank official had a few words with her. He stayed chatting with Father Mitrega as the woman vanished. She was back shortly carrying a tray filled with what looked like thousand dollar bills.

Benjy squeezed his brother's arm hard. 'Here comes the mail, baby!'

The movement below was confusing, people coming and going. It was difficult to keep track of any one person. The three bank guards were all standing near the entrance. There was still no indication that Munro was in the building.

'*Shit!*' Benjy said furiously and leaned out as far as he dared. Munro's two women were crossing the banking

hall. They joined the line at the cage next to the priest.
They smiled across at one another without speaking.

'They're cashing travellers cheques,' said Sheldon. 'I can
see them in their hands.'

The teller was in her cage now with the tray of thousand
dollar bills in front of her. Benjy watched as Mitrega
opened his bag, stacking away the bills as the teller
counted them. The bank official shook Mitrega's hand and
the priest turned, heading for the street, his hat in one
hand, the bag in the other. A guard followed a discreet ten
paces behind him. Suddenly Mitrega sank to his knees,
dropping the things he was carrying, both arms outstretched in front of him as though fending off an unseen
assailant. Then he keeled over sideways. A hysterical
scream sounded above the general hubbub. The two
women from the *Skagerrak* were running across the hall
towards the stricken priest.

Benjy could feel himself paling. 'The bastard's dropped
dead on us!' he gasped.

They raced down the marble stairway, slithering in their
haste to reach the bottom. Startled faces recoiled as Benjy
thrust his way through the crowd that had gathered about
the recumbent priest.

'Stand back!' he bawled, using his shoulders vigorously.
He could see Mitrega's bag lying on the floor. A bank guard
loomed. Benjy called to him. 'Make these people stand
back, I've had medical training!'

The bank guard cleared space for him. The older woman
was on her knees beside the priest with her shopping basket
on the ground next to her. Mitrega was lying on his back,
breathing stertorously. Benjy inserted a finger in the
priest's collar and wrenched it open. The priest's eyes
stared up without recognition. Someone stuck a glass of
water in Benjy's hand. He held it to Mitrega's lips. Sheldon
had stepped over the priest's bag and was backheeling it
through the crowd towards the exit.

'It's me,' Benjy urged. 'Everything's going to be all right.
Try to drink this water!'

Mitrega was dribbling weakly. 'Shouldn't we take out his dentures?' It was the older woman, her face anxious as she looked at Benjy.

The idea repulsed him. 'Later,' he said. He helped the priest to his feet. Mitrega shook his head, looking around the ring of faces with bewildered eyes. He started to refasten his collar with shaking fingers.

A bank guard beat his palms together. 'It's all over, folks! Let's move it along here now!'

The crowd started to disperse. Sheldon had vanished. 'The bag!' the younger woman said suddenly, looking round. 'Father Mitrega's bag!'

The smile froze on Benjy's face. He grabbed the priest's arm. 'Tell her it's all right,' he said in a savage undertone.

The women followed them to a nearby bench. The corners of the priest's lips were flecked with white. He used Benjy's handkerchief to wipe away the flecks.

'It's all right,' he said with difficulty, looking up at the two women. 'My friend is taking care of the bag. Everything is all right, God bless you!'

The crowd had completely dispersed, figures moving about the hall again like clockwork toys that had been rewound. Benjy leaned heavily on his charm.

'I'm pretty sure that this is nothing serious. The thing to do is get him back to the boat and have the doctor look at him. The trouble is that I can't accompany you. I have to be somewhere else.'

He suddenly wanted out. The man in the seersucker suit was talking to one of the bank guards and looking in their direction. The older woman nodded understanding. She picked up her shopping basket and hooked an arm under the priest's. Her companion took his other arm.

'We'll take care of him!'

'No liquor!' warned Benjy and touched the priest's shoulder. 'I'll see you later, Father!'

He made it fast to the street, the small of his back electric with apprehension. But the shots and shouts sounded only in his head. It was quiet outside. Sheldon had the engine of the Chrysler ticking over. Benjy sprinted across the pavement and hurled himself into the passenger seat.

'Get this motherfucker *moving!*'

He reached behind with one hand, groping for the bag on the back seat. It was locked and the priest still had the key. No matter. Time enough to break it open later. A man in a yellow pickup veered sharply as Benjy let out a whoop of triumph.

'Goddamn, Shel, we've done it! Five hundred big ones, like taking pennies from a blind man's cup!'

Sheldon was driving east on Baldorioty de Castro, watching his rearview mirror narrowly.

'Where the hell was Munro?'

Benjy straightened his jacket. 'Who the hell knows? He could have been inside the bank and walked out when he saw the commotion. Or he could be around the block somewhere, sitting there waiting for us to bring the loot to him.'

'I don't like it,' said Sheldon. 'Why don't we find someone with a boat and forget about Spinoza.'

Benjy laid a soothing arm along the back of Sheldon's seat. 'Take it easy, kid. Everything's cool. Hey, you were great! Moving that goddamn bag back like a soccer player dribbling a ball.'

For once Sheldon's smile looked as if it meant something. 'People were stepping over, Benjy. I'd say excuse me and they'd move!'

'Take a left,' Benjy said suddenly.

Sheldon spun the wheel. It was five minutes past three when they reached the terminal building. Spinoza was there driving a big black Lincoln.

Sheldon's mouth twisted. 'All he needs is a violin case.' He swung the Chrysler in behind as the Lincoln glided away past hangars and maintenance sheds onto a service road that skirted the airfield. A dozen or so private craft were parked in the north-west corner. A long distance jet was taxying out to the main runway, its tyres leaving streaks on the warm tarmac. The sun was brilliant in an azure sky. The windsock flew at right angles to its pole. The Lincoln stopped close to a small sleek plane. A tall man wearing cowboy boots and a baseball cap came across to meet Spinoza. A couple of large henchmen were doing their best to make themselves inconspicuous behind the plane.

Sheldon stopped the Chrysler fifty yards away. A rush of well-being hit Benjy in sensitive places.

'Tell me,' he said, grinning.

'Tell you what?' asked Sheldon.

Benjy's smile widened. 'That your brother's a genius.'

'You're a genius.' Sheldon reached back and collected the bag.

'Give it to me,' said Benjy. No way would he share this moment. He put the bag on the floor, grabbed the lip of the lid with his fingers and heaved. The first time it held. He put his feet on the bag and tried again. The lock gave with a loud report, causing the pilot and Spinoza to look in their direction. Benjy lifted the broken lid. The interior of the bag was filled with newspaper cut to the size of thousand dollar bills.

Benjy looked up. His mouth had gone completely dry. Old bad memories were trying to break loose from his head. The white buildings and control tower danced as though seen in a mirage. He flicked through the piles of cut newsprint and gulped hard.

'We've been had,' he said blankly.

'Had,' Sheldon repeated as though mesmerized.

'They pulled a Murphy on us,' said Benjy.

Sheldon shook his head and swallowed. Spinoza and his friends had left the airplane and were strolling across to the Chrysler. The gold cross around Spinoza's neck glinted in the sunlight.

'What do we do, Benjy?' Sheldon was very much lost at that moment.

Benjy plastered a grin on his face for the oncoming

trouble. 'I just ran out of ideas,' he said. 'But I can tell you one thing. It's no time for long speeches.'

FOURTEEN

Drury was still perched on the rear end of the Cadillac, his binoculars trained on the bank entrance. The Californians had left their Chrysler on the parking lot across the street. Drury checked his watch. Twenty-eight minutes had passed since Russell had gone in. The length of time suggested that Russell had cleared the first hurdle. Disaster would have struck within the first few minutes. Not only that, neither Emily-May nor Judy had appeared with the prearranged signal. In the event of trouble, the plan called for Russell to sit tight. His defence would be a mixture of fact and fiction, an account of a guileless priest in the hands of two sophisticated rogues. A few shrewdly placed telephone calls would end the charade but with any kind of luck Russell would have got bail before that happened. Twenty thousand dollars had been earmarked for the purpose.

Drury shifted the binoculars fractionally as a couple leaving the bank stopped in their tracks at the top of the steps outside. The woman was pointing back behind her. The couple retraced their steps. It was clear that something was going on in the banking hall. Drury wet his lips. More than anything at that particular moment he needed a smoke. He fished a cigar from his pocket, one handed, and lit it, still holding the binoculars. *Thirty-one minutes.* If things were going the way he hoped he'd see evidence of it at any moment.

Smoke drifted across the lens and he shifted the cigar from one side of his mouth to the other. His fingers gripped tight and he panned. The younger of the two Californians had burst through the glass doors. He forced himself into a slow saunter that took him across the street to the parked Chrysler. He threw the black bag he was carrying on the back seat and slid behind the wheel. A puff of smoke in the thin air showed that the engine had been started. Drury panned back to the bank entrance. *Thirty-eight minutes.* What the hell was happening in there! Surely the others hadn't blown it at this stage in the game!

Adrenalin raced again as the red-head emerged from the bank. There was no pretence of a casual saunter. The red-head charged across to the parking lot and hurled himself into the seat next to his partner. The Chrysler barged forward, narrowly missing a motor-cyclist. Stop lights ahead forced the driver to slow. A green light released the traffic and the Chrysler disappeared. Five minutes later, Russell emerged from the bank supported by Emily-May and Judy. Emily-May was still carrying her straw shopping basket. Drury could see a bank guard peering out through the glass as the trio descended the steps.

He replaced the binoculars in their case and hurried down to street level. He started the Dodge, paid the parking dues and drove out to meet the others. Russell's collar had been removed and his lips still bore traces of dried sherbet foam. He climbed into the back seat beside Emily-May. Judy was next to her father. Drury indicated the bag of clothes at Russell's feet.

'Get those things on fast! And leave that passport in the pocket of your other clothes!'

He put the gears in low and joined the eastbound traffic. By the time they reached the first set of haltlights Russell had his trousers off. Emily-May shielded him from the other cars as he completed his change. Drury glanced sideways at Judy, wanting her to share his euphoria. She looked at him strangely, as a child who sees her first rabbit produced from a hat might. Then she smiled. His eyes sought the rearview mirror. Emily-May was sitting bolt upright, Russell's discarded clothing across her lap. She made a bundle of it and held up Russell's false passport. Then she slipped it in the pocket of the clerical jacket.

'Good girl,' Drury said over his shoulder. 'Now show us the loot!'

She removed the paper vegetables from her basket and took out the black bag that was concealed beneath. The dimensions were half-an-inch smaller than the bag taken by the Californians otherwise the bags were identical. Drury throttled down as they reached the causeway, still using the rearview mirror. Emily-May sprang the locks and lifted the lid of the bag. Thousand dollar bills filled the interior.

Drury beat his fist on the steering wheel. 'We *made* it, folks!'

Nobody spoke but the answer was there on every face. Emily-May closed the bag again and glanced sideways at Russell.

'Olivier here was magnificent!'

Russell shot his cuffs and tried to look modest. 'I was magnificent,' he admitted.

Drury checked his watch again. His life at the moment was measured in minutes.

'We're running it close. We've got twenty-five minutes to make the plane.'

There was nothing behind. The nearest car coming from the opposite direction was a quarter of a mile away. He braked and anchored the bundle of clothing to the bottom of the lagoon with a rock. They reached Isla Verde with eleven minutes to spare before take-off. Drury left the keys in the rented car. Each of them had his flight ticket.

'We meet on the plane and *move* it!'

They hurried across the concourse, Drury carrying the bag. He was last of the four to arrive at the desk. The girl there exchanged his ticket for a boarding pass, her hand already reaching for the phone.

'You'll have to hurry, sir. The last call was five minutes ago.'

A khaki-uniformed official waved Drury through and he

ran for the boarding shuttle. The bulky door closed behind him and the steps were removed. There was a seat next to Judy. Emily-May and Russell were in the row behind. Drury put the bag and binoculars in the overhead rack. A couple of hostesses were talking down the aisle, checking seat-belts. The captain's voice sounded in the tannoy. Half a dozen small aircraft were parked in the north-west corner of the airfield, half a mile away. The jet gathered speed and lifted off. There was a clunk as the undercarriage locked home on closed position. The captain's voice had been replaced by the sound of Herb Alpert.

Drury twisted in his seat, holding tight to Judy's hand. 'What do you say, Champ?'

'What do I say?' Russell's fat face widened in an enormous grin. 'I say there's only a few of us left!'